Cinnamon Girl

Starting
Over

Cathy Hopkins is the author of the incredibly successful *Mates, Dates* and *Truth, Dare* books, and has now started a fabulous new series called *Cinnamon Girl*. Cathy lives in North London with her husband and three cats, Maisie, Emmylou and Otis.

Cathy spends most of her time locked in a shed at the bottom of the garden pretending to write books but is actually in there listening to music, hippie dancing and talking to her friends on email.

Occasionally she is joined by Maisie, the cat who thinks she is a copy-editor and likes to walk all over the keyboard rewriting and deleting any words she doesn't like.

Emmylou and Otis are new to the household. So far they are as insane as the older one. Their favourite game is to run from one side of the house to the other as fast as possible, then see if they can fly if they leap high enough off the furniture. This usually happens at three o'clock in the morning and they land on anyone who happens to be asleep at the time.

Apart from that, Cathy has joined the gym and spends more time than is good for her making up excuses as to why she hasn't got time to go.

Cathy Hopkins

Cinnamon Girl

Starting Over

PICCADILLY PRESS * LONDON

As this book is essentially about friends, I'd like to dedicate this one to Anne O'Malley who's been my friend since I was thirteen when, like India Jane in this book, I had to start a new school and was dreading it. And thanks, as always, to Brenda Gardner, Anne Clark, Melissa Patey and all the fab team at Piccadilly.

First published in Great Britain in 2007
by Piccadilly Press Ltd,
5 Castle Road, London NW1 8PR
www.piccadillypress.co.uk

Text copyright © Cathy Hopkins, 2007

A catalogue record for this book is available from the British Library

ISBN: 978 1 85340 916 5 (trade paperback)

1 3 5 7 9 10 8 6 4 2

Printed in the UK by CPI Bookmarque, Croydon, CR0 4TD
Text design by Carolyn Griffiths, Cambridge
Cover design by Simon Davis
Cover illustration by Sue Hellard

Chapter 1

Starting Over

'MUUUM, have you seen my rucksack?' I called down from my bedroom on the third floor.

'MUM, where's the shoe polish?' my brother, Dylan, called from the bathroom on the second floor.

'Both in the cupboard under the stairs and both of you, GET A MOVE ON!' Mum shouted up from the ground floor. 'I have better things to do with my time than chase the two of you to do something you should have done AGES AGO.'

'It's only last-minute stuff, I'm almost there,' I called back.

I slid down two flights of banisters to the first floor then took the stairs to the ground, but I wasn't feeling as carefree as I appeared. Not by a long shot. The next day was going to be the start of term at a new school and I'd be going into Year Eleven.

'Ah, what vision of loveliness is this?' I asked when I spotted Mum's backside in the air as she scrabbled about on her knees with her head in the cupboard under the stairs. She located my rucksack and pulled it out from the tangle of bags and cases stuffed in the cupboard, then began to crawl out. 'Thanks,' I said as I took it from her.

'Looking forward to tomorrow?' she asked as she knelt back, loosened her auburn hair then twisted it up again into a bun.

'About as much as a visit to the dentist's.'

Mum stood up and dusted off the peacock-blue velvet top she was wearing over her jeans. It never ceased to amaze me how even after fishing about in a dirty old cupboard she still managed to look lovely – like a princess out of an Edward Burne-Jones Pre-Raphaelite painting. 'You'll be fine, India Jane,' she said. 'You've done it so many times before.'

'Yes and *each* time has been more difficult. You don't understand. Starting a new school is not something that gets easier. It gets harder.'

'Well it will be new for Dylan too,' said Mum as he appeared on the stairs in his pyjamas, his rust-brown hair slicked down wet and his face fresh and pink from his bath.

'Yeah —' he started.

'Oh, he'll be OK,' I interrupted. 'Everyone going into Year Seven will be new. All the dinky little kids are in the same situation, little fish in the big pond. They can be wide-eyed and anxious together. They can bond over it. But going into Year Eleven, I'll probably be the *only* new girl in my year.'

2

Dylan walked over and punched my arm. 'Less of the dinky little kid, dingbat-brain.'

'Dingbat-brain, huh? And you? You are a bug on the windscreen of my life, O small-but-annoying one, and you know what happens to them.' In a flash, I dropped my rucksack, flicked out my right leg, hooked it around his left, grabbed his torso and pushed him to the floor. It was an ace move. I had learned in a self-defence class at my last school. I rested my left foot on his stomach and began to sing, 'I am the champion, *I am the champion . . .*'

He reached up and karate-chopped the back of my knee.

'Owwwwww!'

'Stop it, you two!' said Mum. 'For heaven's sake, India, act your age.'

'I am. I'm fifteen. You're always telling me not to grow up too fast. Make up your mind.'

Dylan pushed me off, scrambled to his feet and stuck his tongue out. 'Boys don't like tomboys,' he said, 'so you'll never get a boyfriend.'

'Says who? And how do you know I haven't already got one?'

'You wish,' said Dylan. He turned away from us, wrapped his arms around himself and started wriggling in a suggestive way so that, from our position, it looked as if someone had their arms around him. He started making slurpy kissing noises. 'Oh Joe, *Joe . . .*'

I raced over and put my hands around his neck. 'God help any girl that you try and kiss,' I said as I began to strangle him,

3

then tried to wrestle him down to the ground. 'You sound like you're slurping noodles.'

'Muuuuum, she's attacking me again. Muu-*uuuum*.'

Mum watched us for a few seconds then sighed. 'India, put your brother aside,' she said wearily. 'He's not a toy. And you'll both be fine tomorrow at school although . . . sometimes I wonder if we *should* have stayed in one place instead of trawling all over the world. Maybe we should have let you have a normal family life.'

I let go of Dylan and he went to look in the cupboard under the stairs, but not before elbowing me in the stomach as he went past.

'Yes. We should have stayed in one place, Mum,' I said. 'As it is, I am scarred for life and will need years of therapy when I'm older.'

'You need it now,' said Dylan over his shoulder. 'But I doubt any psychotherapist could help you.'

Mum laughed. She knew I was joking. Kind of. Part of me was serious and wished I had experienced the usual upbringing. One junior school. One secondary. The same best friends since Year Seven. *Especially* the same-best-friends-since-Year-Seven bit. Being on my own tomorrow and going into a year where all the friendships and cliques would have been well established years ago – that was the part I was dreading the most. My family had been on the move since I was born and I'd already lived in five different countries – Rajasthan in India, St Lucia in the Caribbean, Venice in Italy, Essaouria in Morocco, Dingle Bay in

4

Ireland – all wonderful places: the wing of an ancient palace (the rest of it was a hotel), a lovely colonial house, an old palazzo, a villa and a derelict castle. Mum and Dad loved travelling. And we did see some extraordinary sights and have experiences I wouldn't swap for anything, but all I ever really wanted was a proper home. And a bunch of good mates. Not that I don't have friends. I do, but I feel like I have spent my whole life saying goodbye to them when my family have moved on.

At last, it looked like we might be staying in one place for a while now that we were in Holland Park in my aunt's house (apart from Dad). Mum and Dad ran out of funds (i.e. Mum's inheritance) about a year ago so had needed to rethink the plan. Due to the lack of cash, Dad had taken the first job he could – and was still travelling, but only until October when he was going to come back to join us. He was with an orchestra who were on tour in Europe, and I did miss him. Even though there were five of us living at Aunt Sarah's and a constant stream of visitors, the house felt quiet without his larger-than-life presence. Apart from that, the rethink turned out well. Aunt Sarah's house is awesome with five floors, so plenty of room for all of us. And she has the best taste – at least I like it. Airy light rooms with tall bay windows, wooden floors, (with underfloor heating which is sooo fab after some of the leaky, freezing places we've lived in), warm soft colours on the walls, lots of interesting ethnic art and nick-nacks from her travels in the Far East. Totally tasteful, but then that's Aunt Sarah. The only truly crap part about the move was leaving my best friend, Erin, in Ireland at the beginning of summer. That was an awful wrench.

'Have you spoken to Erin?' Mum asked, picking up on my thoughts. 'She always cheers you up.'

I shook my head. 'I tried to call her before. She's not in. Her school starts the day after ours, so no doubt she's out making the most of it.'

'Or out snogging that poser, Scott Malone,' said Dylan as he crawled out of the cupboard with the shoe-polish box.

'How do you know about him?' I asked. 'Have you been reading my emails?'

Dylan rolled his eyes. 'As if. I am quite particular about the quality of fiction I read.'

'How else would do you know about him? Mum, I *really* need my own computer.'

'You should be glad that there's only two of you sharing that one up in your room and glad that Sarah had no use for it when she upgraded. If it wasn't for her, we'd all have to use the one in my workroom and we'd *all* be reading your emails.'

'Her emails are quite good for a laugh,' Dylan said, then continued in a girlie voice, 'I can't wait to see Joe again at school tomorrow. I think we really connected in Greece . . .'

'Right! That's it, you little perv. You're a dead man.' I made a dive for Dylan and decided to go for his weak spot. He's very ticklish. I got him back on the floor and tickled him mercilessly under his arms.

He squealed like a baby. 'Mu-*uuuuuuuum*!'

Mum sighed again then walked around us as if we weren't there. 'Supper in twenty minutes,' she said as she went through the door to the kitchen.

I released Dylan, who rolled over on to his side and got up. 'And I don't want you tagging along with me tomorrow,' he said as he followed Mum into the kitchen. 'I don't want you cramping my style.'

'*What* style?' I asked as I headed back upstairs. 'Sometimes I *so* wish I had sisters.'

'So do I,' Dylan called after me. 'Or at least a sister who knew how to behave like a GIRL!'

After supper, I went up to my bedroom, got out a sheet of paper and made a list.

Good things about starting new school:
1) Kate: she's my cousin.

We live in her house. Well not her house, her mum's. My Aunt Sarah's. Unlike my mum, who blew her inheritance, Aunt Sarah cannily invested hers, made tons of dosh and has this fabbie house in Holland Park. She's divorced and, as there was only her and Kate living here, she said we could stay here until Mum and Dad get sorted. (Which will be never. I know how much houses cost in London. Squillions. And then some. And I also know that when it comes to money, Mum and Dad are Peter Pan and Wendy. Not grown up yet. So I reckon we'll be staying with dear Aunt Sarah for quite some considerable time – which luckily she seems very happy about.) Kate'll be going into Year Thirteen tomorrow, her last year. She's been at the school since Year Seven, which means she knows all there is to know about the place, plus she is über-cool and bound to be well respected there. We hung out over the summer and I am sure she will show me round and introduce me to anyone worth knowing.

2) Joe: he's the boy I met in Greece.

Dylan is right, we do have a connection – more than that. I have an almighty great crush on him as he is the most gorgissimus boy I have ever met, as well as being funny in a cool, dry way. And he's interesting and into art like I am. A love affair is clearly meant to be, I reckon, he just has to agree to it too! His mum, Lottie, and my Aunt Sarah run a New Age centre on Skiathos. I spent the summer there and got to know him a little. He wasn't at the centre all the time because he had a holiday job down in the local village, but when he was there, there was definitely chemistry in the air and when we said goodbye at the airport after we'd flown back from Greece together, things were positively sizzling. We would have had our first snog if there hadn't been a million other people in the waiting area, including our respective relatives who were there to pick us both up. I can't wait to hook up with him now that we're back in England – in fact, I was hoping that he might have been in touch before we started term, but we've not even been back a week so I guess he had stuff to do as he will be going into his last year and doing A-levels, same as Kate.

3) I can walk to the school from here.

Twenty minutes tops, so that's good.

4) I already have a contact to look out for in my year. A girl called
Leela.

Her sister Anisha works for Aunt Sarah. I met her in Greece and before I left she told me to look out for her sister. If she's anything like Anisha, she'll be well grooved up.

Bad things about starting school:
1) Don't know anyone apart from Kate, Joe, Leela (and I don't
even know her yet) and Dylan.
2) I have to pick up my GCSE subjects halfway through the
syllabus and, because it is slightly different to my last school, there
will be a lot of catching up to do to keep up with the others.
3) New teachers.
4) Having to wear school uniform. Black-and-white this time.

OK, so you get a choice of skirt style – I chose pencil-straight, but it looks so drab and how am I supposed to wow Joe Donahue when I'm dressed like a penguin?

Tactics for starting school:
1) Lie low.
2) Observe.
3) Don't draw attention to myself until I know what's what
and who's who. And even then, don't draw attention to myself.

4) Arrive on time in the morning. Don't hang about in the afternoon.

5) Go in with Kate and be seen with her as often as possible so that people will think I am as cool as she is.

Essentials to take:
1) Book, so that if I am ever on my own, I can pretend to be doing something.
2) Natural lip-gloss, for Joe Donahue sightings.
3) Mobile, for texting Erin as often as possible.

After I'd written down my tactics, I decided to have a last try-on of the uniform. As I have chestnut-red hair and amber eyes, black and white are not the most flattering colours on me and can make me look washed out. I could just get away with it as I still had a good tan from my time in Greece, but normally I look better in autumn or spice-colour shades. Dad calls me Cinnamon Girl because of my colouring (but also because one of his favourite songs by Neil Young has that title).

Just as I was experimenting to see how much make-up I might get away with, Erin called. 'Hey,' she said. 'I decided to call instead of text as, knowing you, you'll be getting yourself all worked up into a tizz and need to hear from me, the voice of sanity, wisdom and sense.'

'You? The voice of sanity and sense? Are you on drugs?'

'Cheek. I'll go then, shall I?'

'Noooo. Thanks for calling. You're a pal, Erin. I *do* need to talk to you. Where you been?'

'Ah, to a movie with some of the girls.'

'Not Scott?'

'Not Scott. You know what he's like. "Commitment" to him is snogging with tongues, and that he does with a number of girls. I don't know if I want to be just one on his ticklist, no matter how cute he is.'

'No. You deserve him all to yourself.'

'Exactly. So, are you worried about tomorrow? On a scale of one to ten . . .'

'Fifteen.'

'Ah you'll be fine, India Jane. You're a Gemini. They're the best sign for making new mates.'

'Not in Year Eleven.'

'Don't worry. You still have me. So what you doing?'

'Getting ready. Trying on the uniform.'

'Black-and-white, isn't it?'

'Yeah. Black skirt. White shirt. So far, I've tried the shirt with sleeves rolled up, down. One button loose, tie loose . . .'

'How about wearing the shirt back to front like a mad person, wear your tie around your leg and put your knickers over your head for a *totally* individual look?'

'*So* glad you called. I knew I could rely on you for sensible suggestions.'

'Can you wear your own shoes?'

'Nope. Black loafers are compulsory.'

'Mmm – sexy. Not.'

'I know. I'd have worn my Converse All Stars if I could.'

'Ah but you'll see the gorgeous Joe.'

'I will.'

'Text me immediately on spotting him. *Immediately*, you hear? You're so lucky to be going to a mixed school, whereas I have to go back to the nunnery.'

'Wish I was there with you, Erin.'

'Me too. I wish I was there with you, although – hold on a mo.'

'What?'

'Remember what that holy chap said, the one whose meditation classes you did in Greece . . .'

'Sensei. What did he say?'

'You told me that he said that we shouldn't always wish to be somewhere we're not. We have to be here and now.'

'Wow, you've got a good memory, Erin. And I thought you weren't interested in what he had to say. I thought you were worried that he was going to scoop out my soul and eat it with a raspberry coulis.'

'Well that just shows how little you know me, India Jane Ruspoli. I am a woman of depth and mystery, as well as wise and sensible and generally marvellous.'

'And modest.'

'Of course,' said Erin. 'But actually, I thought that your man spoke a lot of sense. It's mad that you want to be here and I want to be there. We should try and make the most of where we are.'

I was surprised at Erin's turnaround because in the summer, when I'd got into meditation, she had been *really* sniffy about it, like I'd joined a cult run by aliens. 'OK. Cool. Be here now.

12

Groovy. Love and peace. Like, yeah baby yeah.'

'Don't you take the pissola now, you eejit. Clearly the purity of your soul has been corrupted by your short stay in London, but I shall pray for you. Ah but you know what I mean. What I am trying to say is let's make the most of it and be positive.'

'You sound like my mum, and you know what an old hippie she is.'

'So? Nothing wrong with that. Yeah, love and peace and good vibes to everyone. And it will soon be half-term and I'll be there.'

'Can't wait.'

'Me neither. So, carry on with your trying-on sesh. Have your lip-gloss at the ready. And remember, India, you're a fab and gorgeous girl and anyone would be honoured to be your friend. Seriously. I'll never forget how totally brilliant you were when my ma had her breast cancer scare.'

'Anyone would have done the same.'

'Not necessarily. Some people run away when people are ill, especially when they hear the word "cancer", like they can't handle it. You were always there for me and I'll never forget that.'

'Well, you're my mate. I care about you and your ma. How's she doing?'

'Just great. Still enjoying being back at work. She looks good.'

'Give her my love.'

We carried on our conversation for another ten minutes and she gave me the gossip on everyone I used to know over in Ireland, then I had a shower and got ready for bed. I felt marginally better after talking to Erin, especially when I imagined going in the school gate with my shirt on back to front and my knickers on my head. Then I remembered a technique that Dad said he used when he felt nervous about performing (he's a musician as well as other things). He said he imagined his audiences wearing something clownish. I decided to combine Dad's method with Erin's and imagined everyone − all the unknown faces I would meet tomorrow, all the teachers, all the pupils, *all* of them − with their knickers on their heads. The anxiety scale fell to five. *Now, think nice thoughts,* I told myself as I remembered Erin's advice to be positive as I snuggled down under my duvet. Images of Joe Donahue immediately came to mind and I felt an immediate warm honey sensation in my stomach as my imagination played a dozen romantic reunions through my mind: Joe and I hand in hand going into school. Crowds of pupils in awe that the new girl had got off with the cutest boy in the school. Joe and I playing the lead roles in *Romeo and Juliet* and him insisting that we rehearse the snogging scenes *a lot.* Joe and I laughing, chatting at lunch break, clearly so in love − again watched by envious admirers. Joe teaching me French. Me reading him poetry. Joe and I in the art room, having fun, having a paint fight. Joe and I running for the school team − joint winners. Joe and I. Joe and I. *So weird,* I thought, *all these feelings going through me today. Anxiety about starting over tomorrow − that's a sour feeling. Then I think of Joe Donahue and it's sweet. Sweet and sour. I am clearly in the Chinese-takeaway phase of my life.*

14

Chapter 2

First Day

'So,' said Dylan as we made our way to school the next morning, 'it's really important that we check out the quality of the canteen. Do they do junk food or do they do celebrity-TV-chef-type nosh? If junk, we take packed lunches. Right?'

'Dylan . . .'

'Yeah?'

'Put a sock in it.'

Mornings have never been my best time and it had been a rude awakening to be reminded that there are two seven o'clocks in the day. One nice one (in the evening) and one *horrid* one first thing. I was going to miss being able to sleep in, it was one of the best perks of holidays.

Dylan's face betrayed the tiniest hurt and I realised that, behind his bravado act, he was as nervous as I was. He always rambled when he was worried about something. Actually he also rambled when he wasn't. Dylan could talk for England, but he could charm too. He was a sweet kid with an appealing face and he looked so cute in his uniform with his black-and-yellow tie done up. He'd make a pile of mates in no time. I regretted being sharp with him. It wasn't his fault we had to go to a new school or that I had been dragged from under my cosy duvet and out into this wet September day.

About a metre before we reached the main road that led to our school, Dylan suddenly put his hand up to his mouth, turned towards a wall, bent over, gagged and threw up.

'Ohmigod! Dylan are you OK?' I went over and put my hand on his back.

After a few moments, Dylan straightened up, nodded and looked around anxiously. 'Nobody saw me did they? Nobody in the same uniform?'

I followed his gaze around the area. 'No. Only me. Don't worry.'

Poor, poor Dylan, I thought as I looked at his pale face and watering eyes. 'Are you OK?'

He nodded shakily. 'Got a tissue?'

I pulled one out of my pocket. 'Do you want to go home?'

He shook his head. 'You *sure* no one saw?' he asked as he wiped his mouth.

'No one,' I said and I gave him a hug. 'And no one saw that either. You'll be fine, Dylan Ruspoli. Everyone going into your year is going to be anxious. There will be kids throwing up all over Notting Hill today. It's going to be puke city . . .'

Dylan pulled a face. 'Ergh, India, visual overload.'

'I'm just trying to say that you're not alone. And I bet you, give it half a day and everyone's going to be queuing up to be your friend. Secondary school is a gas.'

'Oh really? So why are you Miss Doom and Gloom even more than you usually are this morning?' he asked as he pulled on my arm to indicate we should walk on.

'I'm not,' I said, although, actually, I was *Queen* of Doom and Gloom. I was feeling miserable – and not just because of the early rise. It was because of Kate. My lovely, compassionate, sensitive, warm-hearted cousin. Not. When we were having breakfast earlier that morning, I had asked if I could go in with her. She had put down her toast, sighed as if she had the weight of the world on her shoulders then given me a long speech about 'stuff' she had to do on the way, *plus* she was meeting up with her mate Chloe, *plus* she was going in later today as Sixth Formers had different schedules – and *oh* the pressure of A-levels, stress, all too much. I think she must have seen my face fall (I'm not very good at hiding my feelings) because she then tried to backtrack with some spiel about me needing space and that I needed to find my own set of friends and identity, blah de blah de blah. She was blowing me off and we both knew it. I knew what it was like in schools. Sixth Formers simply don't mix with the younger years.

As we turned into the road that led to the school, my phone bleeped that I had a text message. It was from Erin.

Rmembr to smile; of all the things u wear, it's the mst imprtant.

That's sweet, I thought, *and a good job that she'd texted as I might have forgotten to turn my phone off.* It would have been so embarrasing if it had gone off in my first assembly. I was about to turn it off when it bleeped another message. This time she'd written:

Don't smile 2 much tho or peeps will thnk ur a loonie.

I laughed. *Thanks for the advice, Erin,* I thought, then I switched it off and stashed it in my rucksack.

The traffic became more congested as we got closer to the school. Fleets of four-wheel drives and people carriers were double parked, horns blared from cars who were held up behind them and couldn't get through, and droves of pupils in black-and-white uniforms were swarming towards the school from all directions, some getting out of cars, others off buses, a few on bicycles, others, like Dylan and I, arriving by foot. I felt my stomach lurch with nerves as the noise level grew as old friends greeted each other, linked arms and headed in through the gates. I turned to glance at Dylan. 'OK?' I asked.

He nodded but he still looked pale. 'Got any fags?' he asked.

'Dylan! I know you don't smoke.'

'Thought I might start,' he said. 'That and drinking hard liquor.'

That made me laugh as Dylan is Mr Healthy. He reads all the labels on everything, looking for hidden preservatives. For a brief moment, I felt protective and tender towards him, as I could see that he was trying to put me at ease as much as I was trying to reassure him. And then he turned from white to green.

'Oh God . . .' he gasped and ran back in the direction that we'd come from.

I looked towards the school. We'd timed it to perfection so that we weren't too late and weren't too early. I heard the bell go and pupils began to speed up. But there was no way I could go in without Dylan. I turned and raced after him.

To the left of the main road, there was what looked like a quieter road, and that's where he'd gone. I turned the corner and saw him disappear through someone's gate beside a tall privet hedge. I could immediately see why he had done that – a bunch of boys in our uniform were coming along the pavement. I knew that the last thing Dylan wanted was to be seen doing the technicolor yawn on his first day. I walked past the hedge then casually turned into the gateway as if I lived there. I could see Dylan in the corner of the garden, ducked down behind the hedge. I turned back to check the other boys had gone past then looked up and down the street. 'Coast is clear,' I said. 'You going to hurl again?'

Dylan shook his head and came back on to the path. 'Don't think so. Ergh . . . Urghhh . . .' His timing was impeccable. The front door of the house opened and an elderly lady in a hairnet appeared in a long, pink, fleecy dressing gown. She didn't notice us at first because she was looking down at her step. She bent over to pick up her milk and it was *then* that she saw Dylan. She couldn't have missed him really as it was at the exact moment that he lost it and threw up for a third time, all over her front steps.

Her face was a picture. Like she'd seen a ghost. 'Whah . . . Who?' she blustered.

I went into a strange hopping dance behind Dylan. 'Oh God. Oh Lord. I am sooooo sorry. New to the area. Wrong house. So sorry.'

The lady straightened up, pulled her dressing gown tight around her, ducked back in and slammed the door shut. Seconds later, I saw a curtain twitch at the window and she peeped out from behind it.

Poor Dylan was still on his knees.

'Oh bollards. Dylan, are you OK?' I said as I bent over him.

He nodded weakly.

I glanced back at the window and the lady darted back behind the curtain. 'OK, then we need to leg it.'

Dylan got up and hobbled out to the gate then on to the pavement, where we ran to the corner. He was shaking like a leaf. Luckily the street was free of fellow pupils as they had all gone into assembly.

'Take a few deep breaths,' I said and he did as he was told, gasping in gulps of air.

'I'm OK now,' he stuttered, but he still appeared to be shaking. I went to steady him, but when I put my arm around him, he burst out laughing.

'Oh . . . oh,' he wheezed. 'Oh that woman! Oh God. I am sooo sorry. I'll take her some flowers . . . I'll . . . I'll take her a card but . . . but . . . did you see her face?'

'I did. "Freaked out" would be an understatement.'

'She . . . she . . .' Dylan couldn't stop laughing.

I looked around to see if anyone was watching. 'Dylan, are you OK?' I asked. I was seriously worried by his behaviour, but then I remembered about people having hysterics. *Should I slap him like they do in the movies when someone's lost it?* I wondered. 'Dylan, stop laughing. It's not funny.'

'I know but . . . her face . . . and . . .'

And then I began to see the funny side too. Poor lady. A puking schoolboy is not what you expect to find when you open the front door to bring in your milk first thing in the morning. We stood for a while and had to hold our sides from laughing. When we had calmed down, I asked Dylan what he wanted to do.

'Actually I feel a bit better now,' he said as he looked towards the school. 'So come on, let's do it. Let's go in. I don't think I could bear to put it off another day. It would only make this awful feeling last longer.'

'Good man,' I said. 'Plus, I think if that lady found you on her doorstep again tomorrow, she might have a heart attack.'

Dylan nodded. 'I *will* take her flowers. And, India . . .?'

'Yeah?'

'Don't tell anyone, will you? Please. Not Mum or Ethan or Lewis?'

'Course not,' I said. I knew it was hard for Dylan being the youngest sometimes and even though our two elder brothers don't live at home any more, Dylan still felt that he needed to act grown up sometimes.

'Not even when you hate me and could use it against me?'

'I solemnly promise, Dylan. It's our secret . . . although maybe just once when you have the TV remote and there's something I want to watch I might . . .'

Dylan pinched my arm then looked at his watch. 'Holy shitoly! We're late!' he said and then he realised that he hadn't got his bag. 'My rucksack! Shit. Shit. Shit! Where is it? Oh. Oh God, it's under the hedge in that woman's garden! I have to go back.'

He was about to retrace his steps, but I pulled him back. 'I'll go. You stay here.'

I raced back towards the gate just as the skies opened and rain began to lash down. When I reached the hedge on the outside, I did my best to flatten myself against it and edge my way along, the way that spies do in movies. In the distance, I could see someone in a black-and-white uniform was approaching on a bicycle so I quickly darted into the garden, got down on my knees and crawled along by the flowerbed in the hope that if the lady was looking out of the window, she wouldn't see me. I could see the rucksack, and once I had it in my hand I swivelled around, but somehow lost my balance and fell on my back into the flowerbed.

'Drat,' I said as I floundered to get up and wiped the rain dripping from my forehead.

At that moment, a head appeared around the hedge. A familiar head in a black baseball cap.

'Hey, India Jane,' said Joe. 'I thought it was you. You don't live here.'

'Er, no . . . I was . . . just visiting,' I said as I got on to my knees and pulled down the skirt that had ridden up. I indicated the rucksack. 'Left something.'

Joe's eyes filled with amusement. 'Ah. Yes. And in the hedge, I see.'

I tried to get up with as much dignity as I could muster, but my legs were covered with mud and rivulets of water were dripping down my face and nose as the rain continued to fall. 'I . . .'

At that moment, the front door opened and the lady who lived there, who had now got dressed, appeared with a broomstick which she brandished at me. 'Out! Get *out* of my garden right now.' She looked at Joe. 'How many of you are there? You too. Hooligans! Off my property!'

Joe disappeared and I skipped out of the garden, then ran as fast as I could with the lady in pursuit.

'And I'll be reporting you to the school,' she yelled as I hot-footed it down the street, making shooing signs to Dylan who was hovering anxiously on the corner. 'Don't think I won't remember your face.'

'Go, go,' I shouted at Joe, who was back on his bike but was holding back and watching me with concern. 'Go, go . . .'

'Later,' he called over his shoulder and he cycled off and disappeared around the corner with a brief wave at Dylan.

'Later,' I said as I panted round the corner, grabbed Dylan's arm and we ran into the school. *Later*, I thought as my fantasy romantic reunions with Joe smashed into a thousand smithereens.

Chapter 3

First Impressions

'So, how's it going?' asked Erin when I got through to her in morning break. I knew it would cost a fortune to call at that time of day rather than text but it felt like an emergency and I knew I had just about enough phone credit. It was hard to hear her voice above the din in the main hall where all the Year Ten and Elevens were congregated. We had been allowed to stay in because of the torrential rain outside and the noise level was deafening.

'On a scale of one to ten, about minus three,' I said in a loud whisper because I didn't want anyone listening in.

'What? Can't hear you. It sounds like you're in the middle of a railway station.'

'Feels like it too,' I said in a louder voice, then added, 'IT'S TOTAL CRAP.' Unfortunately the last part was at the very

24

moment when everyone in the hall fell simultaneously silent for a nano-second. A hundred pairs of eyes turned to stare at me. I immediately did what my brother Lewis does when he's done a SBD (silent but deadly smell). I looked at a girl sitting next to me as if it had been her who had shouted. She gave me a very strange look back.

'That bad?'

I decided to revert back to whispering. 'I've even got detention.'

'*Detention?* Cool.'

'No, Erin, not cool. It's my first day. I'm supposed to be making a good impression.'

'Yeah, but detention's a great way to meet people, particularly the bad boys, and don't forget that's where I first got off with Scott Malone. So why did you get detention? What did you do?'

'Late.'

'Late? But you only live a short way away and you told me you had timed the journey.'

'Er, yeah . . . I did. Long story. Later.' I didn't want to risk anyone in the hall overhearing the real reason I wasn't on time and I certainly couldn't have told the teacher on late duty who had been hovering like a wasp just inside the school gate. I'd promised Dylan. When neither of us had offered up a good excuse, the teacher had handed us both detention slips, looked at my dripping hair, muddy knees and jacket, and directed us to the main hall with a disapproving frown.

'O-kaaay. Long story. Ohmigod. You saw Joe didn't you? That's why you were late?'

'Er, sort of, no. *Later*, Erin.'

'OK, I got you. You can't talk. OK, so call me as soon as you can, yeah?'

'Yeah. Just needed to check in for a mo, hear a friend's voice, that's all.'

'Gotcha. I can hardly hear you anyway so save your phone credit for when we can speak properly, yeah?'

'I guess,' I said reluctantly.

'Love you loads. Go get 'em girl,' said Erin, and hung up.

I didn't want to hang up as talking to Erin had given me something to do. I was tempted to sit there for a moment and carry on chatting even though there was nobody at the other end, but then I thought that was really sad so I put my phone away and looked around the hall. I shifted about on the bench I was sitting on and did my best to look cool, although I felt awkward and self-conscious, like I had a huge neon sign over my head flashing *NEW GIRL, SHE HAS NO MATES* and an arrow pointing to me. Everyone seemed to know each other because, of course, they did. The majority had been attending school here together for four or five years and were sitting eating crisps, glugging water, juice and Diet Cokes, checking each other out, catching up, laughing, gossiping, all so at ease with their situation and surroundings. I wished Kate or Joe would come along so that I would have someone to talk to, but of course they didn't. The Sixth Formers have their own common room on the third floor.

So far it had been a totally crap morning. After attempting to clean off my legs and muddy jacket in the girls' cloakroom after assembly, one of the prefects who was organising the Year Sevens (hundreds of them) and other newcomers (me) had escorted me to meet my class teacher, Mrs Goldman. She was a big blonde lady with glasses, slightly buck teeth and an enormous bust, but she looked approachable enough and she smelled nice – of strawberries. She was already taking register and thirty heads swivelled to look at me when I walked in the classroom. It was *exactly* the arrival I hadn't planned on as thirty pairs of eyes checked me out while I tried to assume a friendly-but-interesting-and-cool expression. Sadly, trying to convey three different attitudes at the same time was beyond my dramatic prowess. I think I looked more like I'd just sucked on a lemon at exactly the same time as someone had put a pin in my backside. Probably not my best look for making a good first impression. Mrs Goldman introduced me to the class, most of whom had lost interest and turned back to what they were doing after my initial sizing up. I went to the back of the room, where I had the best vantage from which to view my fellow classmates while Mrs Goldman called their names. I took special note when she said, 'Leela Ranjani,' and a pretty Indian girl with a plait on the right of the class answered, 'Here, Miss.'

Not long after the register was over, a bell shrilled, but everyone stayed where they were so that Mrs Goldman could go through everyone's timetable and subjects for the coming year. She paid me extra attention and confirmed that I hadn't changed my mind about the subjects that I'd indicated I wanted to do when I first applied for a place at the school (art, English language, English literature, maths, science, French, RE, media studies, history and music. Ten subjects. Erk!). Plus she told me that I must do at least one after-school activity 'to show a contribution to a group project which could also be counted as part of my coursework'. An after-school activity! On top of ten GCSE subjects! I was hardly going to have time to breathe.

But I liked Mrs G. She seemed comfortably mumsy and genuinely concerned that I settled in all right. After giving me a printout of my timetable and a map of the school, she took me down a maze of corridors and introduced me to my assigned 'buddy' who was to show me around in the second period. Her name was Nicole Hewitt and she was one of those impeccable blondes whose complexion was so milky perfect that she looked like she had been cracked out of styrofoam packaging only that morning. She was clearly a teacher's pet. At first I thought she was going to be a total Goody-two-shoes type, but as soon as we were out of any adult's earshot, she relished the job of filling me in on any gossip on just about everyone who went past.

'See her?' she whispered as a girl with a ton of black kohl round her eyes slouched past. 'Total tart. If you ever like a boy in the school, steer *well* clear of her as she'll have him off you before you can say Bacardi Breezer.'

'See him?' she said when a boy with bleached blond hair sauntered past and gave me a wink. 'My mate Ruby snogged him last year for a dare. Never again. Cheese-and-onion breath. Like, *bleugh* . . . And that guy there?' I followed her glance to see a very cute boy with shoulder-length dark hair at the far end of the corridor. 'Callum Hesketh. Sixth Former. School babe,' she drawled. '*Every*body wants him, but he's very picky . . .' She was fun. Before break, she had shown me all the main areas of the school, plus where the cloakrooms were on different floors (and which ones honked the most and were best avoided), the library (and the best place in there for a sneaky doze or place to text your mates without the librarian seeing – v. useful), staff room (only to be used in emergency or they get v. sniffy and take it out on you later), the canteen, the gym (where apparently Marie Cox, Year Eleven, lost her virginity to Ian Matthews, Year Twelve). *Oo-er, there were none of these types of shenanigans happening at my last school! Least not that I knew about,* I thought as up and down and round and round we walked. After a while, it all became a blur of corridors, doors, windows and stairs. It was a big school with well over a thousand pupils and seemingly endless departments; it would take me years to know my way around. *Someone ought to make a sat-nav for school,* I thought as we hit yet another wing. *They'd make a fortune.*

As soon as the bell went for break, classroom doors opened and in a flash those same empty corridors flooded with a tsunami of teenage bodies of all shapes and sizes. I flattened myself against a wall so as not to get caught up in the surge of activity. I hoped that Nicole would fill me in some more but her phone had bleeped that she had a message, and after she'd checked it she directed me to the hall, shoved me in through the double doors and, with a cheery 'Later,' had left me to it.

I noticed a few boys check me out and a couple of girls looked at me quizzically then turned away as if they found nothing of interest. As I was wondering where to go and sit, I noticed Leela come in behind me. I took a deep breath and plunged in.

'Hey, I know your sister, Anisha. She said to say hi. I'm India Jane.'

'Oh hi,' said Leela with a friendly smile. She was very like her sister, with the same liquid brown eyes and delicate features, but not quite as tall. She was about to say something else when a striking-looking black girl rushed towards her and almost strangled her from behind with a huge bear hug. Leela looked apologetic and shrugged her shoulders as she was dragged away, so I smiled back and shrugged my shoulders too. I wasn't going to follow her like a desperate hanger-on. She clearly had start-of-term catching up to do with a mate, so I went and sat on the opposite side of the room and called Erin. Once I'd hung up, I got out my timetable to glance over in the pretence that I was 'oh, so busy busy' and when I saw that art was my next subject, inspiration struck. The art room. Art was my favourite subject. It was also Joe's favourite subject. There was the slightest chance that he would be in there. Maybe, maybe not, but anything was better than sitting looking like a total saddo.

I asked a boy by the door for directions, first to the area where the Year Sevens would be so that I could check in on Dylan, and then to the art unit. He mumbled which way to go so I set off in the direction that he pointed. After getting totally and completely lost, I bumped into Nicole who was lounging by a radiator with a girl with black hair cut into a sleek bob. She oozed sophistication, which was no mean feat considering she was dressed in school uniform, but somehow she managed to make it look like it was totally stylish.

'Ruby – India Jane . . .' Nicole said.

Ruby arched a perfectly plucked eyebrow and glanced over me. 'Heard all about you,' she drawled. 'First day?'

I nodded. Even though, at five foot eight, I was as tall as her and Nicole, for some reason I felt smaller, immature and like I was a peasant who had come up from the country. Her phone rang and she turned away to answer it and Nicole pulled out her phone and made a call of her own.

As they were chatting, I noticed the cute Sixth Former I'd clocked earlier walk past. Nicole had told me that he was the school babe. It was hard not to notice him as he was probably the best-looking boy I'd seen in the school so far (apart from Joe of course). He saw me glance at him and began to come over. *Probably to talk to Ruby*, I thought as I straightened up and assumed my best cool look.

'New girl,' he said with a nod in my direction as he sauntered past.

I did a double check to make sure that he wasn't talking to

anyone else but no, he was definitely talking to me.

'Actually I'm fifteen,' I replied. 'So not *that* new.'

He laughed and his eyes crinkled up in an appealing way. 'New to the school, I meant,' he said. 'New to me.' When he said that, he looked straight at me and I felt a frisson of chemistry. *Ooh la la*, I thought, *things are looking up*.

He ambled off and Ruby finished her call, looked after him, then back at me. 'Callum Hesketh,' she said flatly.

'Cute,' I said.

She nodded. 'Don't go there.'

'Does he have a girlfriend?'

'Is our headmistress a killjoy? Duh. Get in line if you fancy Callum. He has an entourage of girlfriends.'

'What's he doing around out here when the Sixth Formers have their own common room and canteen?'

Ruby laughed. 'He likes to be seen. Likes to check out the new girls. And most of his admirers are in the younger years so take my advice and don't take him seriously. He's just checking out virgin territory.'

I felt myself blush and hoped that Ruby hadn't noticed. How did she know that I was a virgin?

'Virgin as in new to *him*, I meant,' said Ruby.

(So she *had* noticed me blush.) 'Do *you* fancy him?'

Ruby shook her head. 'Not old enough for me.'

'My friend Erin was into older —' I started, but Ruby hadn't paused for breath.

'Anyhow, been there, got the Callum T-shirt,' she continued.

32

'We dated in Year Eight. Didn't work.'

'Why not?'

'Opposites attract, people that are similar repel. Law of physics. And we can't both be the centre of attention.'

I laughed. Ruby seemed like a laugh. She turned back to Nicole, who was still on her phone. 'Got to go. Laters,' she said and set off down the corridor.

'Laters,' said Nicole as she finished her call.

Without looking back, Ruby gave us a wave over her shoulder. She was clearly the type of girl who was so confident that she knew that people stared after her when she walked away.

Nicole rolled her eyes when Ruby disappeared around a corner. 'Sorry for abandoning you earlier, but Ruby had boy trouble. Had to do urgent counselling. Ruby can't half pick them.'

I was dying to ask more, but thought I'd better not be too nosey on first meeting so instead I smiled. 'No matter. I was fine.'

'So what's next?'

'Art,' I said. 'I was trying to find the art room, and got lost.'

'I've got Spanish, but I'll show you where to go,' said Nicole and she linked arms with me and dragged me off in completely the opposite direction to the way the boy had pointed. *Creep*, I thought, *he was having a laugh at my expense. Yeah. Very funny. Not.*

'So you don't know anybody at the school, hey? That must be really hard . . .'

'No. My kid brother started with me . . .'

'*Kid* brother. Shame.'

'I have others,' I said eagerly. For some weird reason, I found that I wanted to impress Nicole. And her friend Ruby. 'Two older brothers. One is married. That's Ethan, but Lewis isn't. He's a student.' And then I realised that I was offering my brother up like a kid in the playground with sweets, hoping to win favour by having something Nicole wanted. (Mind you, knowing Lewis, he would have been delighted to meet both of them.)

Her eyes did light up when I mentioned him. 'Cool,' she said. 'How old?'

'Nineteen.'

Nicole's eyes were definitely twinkling. 'I'd love to meet him. The boys here are like sooo immature, total write offs, like far too young. Ruby and I prefer students. There are only a couple of decent Sixth Formers here.'

'Oh I know one of them,' I said. 'I mean . . . two of them. Actually my cousin Kate is in the Sixth Form. Kate Rosen.'

Nicole looked slightly impressed. 'Oh yeah. I've seen her around. Tall, black hair, skinny, good cheekbones?'

'Yeah. That's Kate.'

'Her mum's Sarah Rosen, isn't she?"

I nodded.

'Your aunt, then?'

I nodded again.

'Cool. I've read about her in the glossies. And who's the boy?'

'Joe Donahue.'

It was as if I'd said two magic words. Nicole almost fainted.

'Ohmigod. Joe Donahue. How do you know him? Where did you meet him? Come on, tell me all . . .'

'I met him over the summer in Greece at my aunt's . . .'

'In Greece? At your aunt's? Your aunt has a place in Greece as well her shops over here? And Joe was there . . .?' As we made our way to the art room, I felt like I was being interrogated by the police. I shouldn't have worried about asking after Ruby's boyfriend. Nicole was double nosey. She wanted all the details about Joe. Where we met. How many times I saw him. What he was like with me. Did I get off with him? Had he got a girlfriend in Greece? In the end, I wished I had never mentioned Joe. At first, I was trying to impress her by saying that I knew a Sixth Former, but the more she questioned me, the more I found myself holding back. I kept what I told her purposely vague and didn't say anything about having an almighty great crush on him. I wanted to find out what the situation was before I let anyone with such a big mouth into my biggest secrets.

The art room was a large airy room with the usual scattering of easels, drawing boards, portfolios, desks and it smelled of turps and oil paint. It had one wall lined with windows above waist-high cupboards, two walls covered with students' work, and on the fourth wall was a floor-to-ceiling mirror as if at one time it had been used as a dance studio. There was only one other person, a girl, in there – no sign of Joe. Nicole gave the girl a wave and introduced us. 'India Jane, new to the school, this is Mia. She's in our year, different class,' said Nicole. 'OK, toodles. Got to dash.'

Nicole went out, shut the door behind her, and Mia smiled. 'Hey.'

'Hey,' I said. She was about medium height with honey-blond hair cut in layers to her shoulders and had cornflower-blue eyes, freckles and a slightly snub nose. She looked like the kind of girl I'd like to get to know, but she was clearly busy so I decided not to interrupt her. Instead I glanced at the walls where some of the art was displayed.

After looking for a while I saw that, near the door, there was a sheet of paper and a note above it asking people to sign up for scenery-painting for the end-of-term show. *Hmm, I could do that*, I thought. Although portraits were my favourite thing to draw, I could do landscapes, and someone else would be running the show so it would only be a case of doing what I was told, *and* it would count as the extra activity that Mrs Goldman had told me that I had to do. Perfect. I signed up my name below four others.

Mia glanced up as I put my pen away and the bell announced the end of break. 'Scenery-painting?'

I nodded.

'They're doing *The Boy Friend*. You know, all-singing all-dancing . . .'

'I don't know it.'

'Love story. Set in a girls' school in the nineteen-twenties. So how's your first day so far?'

'Yeah. Great. Fine thanks,' I lied. I didn't want to admit that I felt like the odd girl out.

Mia laughed. 'I bet.'

'Well, you know . . .'

'I do actually. Hell probably. I was new last year. It can be a killer coming in after everyone else.'

I breathed a sigh of relief. She really did know what it was like. She beckoned me over to go and sit with her and while the others filed in, she chatted away. I hoped that we could become friends.

When everyone had arrived for the class and settled in, the art teacher arrived: Mr Bailey. He looked like he was in his thirties, not bad-looking for an oldie, with slicked-back hair and a neat beard, and he was wearing a smart black suit and black T-shirt – which I thought was more record producer than art teacher. Bit of a flash git, as Erin would have said if she'd been there. After a short talk about the aims of the next term, he explained that the project until Christmas was to be self-portraits. Someone at the back of class groaned.

'And why the moan, Peterson?' asked Mr Bailey.

'How can I do a self-portrait when I don't know who I am?' a boy with lank brown hair sighed.

'Ah, the blight of teenagers all over the world,' sighed Mr Bailey. 'I suggest that you either cut the angst or *paint* it. See? Maybe this is just the opportunity for you to find out who you are.'

Mr Bailey got a lip-curl sneer by way of a reply from Peterson. I was with Mr Bailey and thought it might be an interesting topic to explore and already had a whole load of images flashing through my head.

'OK, I'm going to make it easy for you, seeing as this is your first day back. First, I want a simple line drawing,' Mr Bailey continued. 'Not too emotive at this point, just a drawing of yourself in the mirror. Detach yourself and just give me the lines in pencil or charcoal.'

I set myself up opposite the mirror next to Mia and soon discovered that Mr Bailey didn't mind if people chatted while they drew, as long as it didn't get too noisy. He called me over before I got properly stuck in and he asked what I had done at my last school and told me what was expected of me this year. He asked me to bring in my portfolio the next day so that he could see what I had done so far, and he seemed pleased that I had already signed up to be a scenery-painter. After that, he left me to it and I sat back with Mia.

We asked each other all the usual questions: where had we lived before? What schools? Friends? Family? And then she asked if I had a boyfriend.

'Not really. I don't know anyone here yet. You?'

Mia nodded. 'We've been dating for about six months, although I didn't see him much over the summer. We had a row at the end of last term. It's all back on though, but, well, you know some boys. You never know where you are . . .'

I nodded and decided that I would tell Mia a little more than I had Nicole, especially as she had been so open with me and I didn't think she seemed the type to use gossip against me or as part of a school tour the way that Nicole had. 'I know, trust is sooo important. And actually . . . there *is* a boy I like but it's early days, but I think we've really connected and they do say that when you feel chemistry that strong then it's always a two-way thing.'

'Exactly,' said Mia.

We both fell quiet for a while as Mr Bailey hovered behind us.

'Nice work, India,' he commented when he glanced over my drawing.

'We must continue this conversation at lunch,' Mia whispered as Mr Bailey sat back on a desk behind us from where he could observe all the drawings. *Cool*, I thought as I continued sketching. *I have made a new friend. Excellent.*

When the bell went for lunch, I got up to go, but Mia asked me to wait for her while she packed up her things. I took the opportunity to have another look at some of the art up on the walls. It looked to be of a high standard and was a mixture of figurative and abstract. In the far corner, above a sink, there was a portrait in charcoal. As I took a closer look, I realised that the style of the artist looked familiar. I leaned in for a closer look. There was Joe's signature at the bottom. Bingo. I'd thought that it was his. I had seen some of his work in the art room in Greece and he had a distinctive way of drawing with strong bold strokes.

Mia came up behind me. 'What do you think of it?'

I nodded then whispered, 'Good. Really good. And . . . actually that's by the boy I was telling you about.'

Mia looked puzzled. 'The boy you were telling me about? What boy?'

'The one I have a crush on, you know, I told you . . .'

Mia's expression froze. 'Joe Donahue?'

I nodded again. 'Do you know him?'

'Oh yes,' she said coldly, then she turned on her heel and left the art room, slamming the door behind her.

Bollards, I thought. *I think I have just found out the name of her boyfriend.*

Chapter 4

Going Home

Dylan and I were the only ones in detention, and the skinny young teacher with blond hair who was supervising looked as if he didn't want to be there any more than we did. He told us to get on with any homework, but as I didn't have any yet, I took the opportunity to revise my list of essentials for starting a new school.

List of good excuses for being late (must make some up and ask Erin and Lewis for some).
Tissues – for blubbing on the way to school.
Water – for after sibling or self has thrown up.
Mints – to sweeten breath when sibling or self has thrown up.
A zip – for a big gob.

I spent the rest of the time doodling some self-portraits, which consisted of me either with an arrow through my head, being hung, or with a gun to my head. It had been that kind of a day. After Mia had left me in the art room, I had waited a few minutes, then made my way to the canteen. As I'd stood in the queue to buy a sandwich and a juice, I'd spotted Mia at a corner table. She'd looked as though she had been crying and two girls were comforting her. One of them was Leela Ranjani. She'd noticed me in the queue then said something to Mia. Mia had nodded and they'd all looked over at me. If looks could kill, I would have been a dead man. I'd turned away, bought my sandwich, then fled the canteen. I'd felt like crying myself. I'd found a spot down a quiet corridor, drank my juice, but didn't touch my sandwich. My appetite had gone. I'd felt sick. Why hadn't Joe told me that he had a girlfriend? Why hadn't Nicole? She seemed to know everybody's business well enough. She could have warned me.

Now in detention, Dylan glanced over at my drawings. 'You're weird,' he whispered. 'Bad day?'

I nodded.

Dylan gave me a sympathetic look. 'I'll buy you some chocolate buttons on the way home.'

After about fifteen minutes, the teacher looked at his watch, made us promise not to be late again and then he let us go early.

On the way home, I called Mum to let her know that we had 'to run an errand for school supplies' and then Dylan and I took a detour to the flower stall near Holland Park tube station, where he used up the rest of his lunch money for that week on buying a bouquet of white tulips (and a packet of chocolate buttons for me). Next stop was back to visit the lady whose doorstep he'd puked all over.

I asked if he wanted me to deliver the flowers or at least go with him, but he insisted on doing it himself and I was relieved to see that he was back to his normal confident self after having 'the most brilliant day ever'. I waited behind the hedge as he went up the path, and when I peeked around after having heard the door open, I witnessed the woman's face change from showing a scowl to suspicion to a smile. Dylan could charm the birds out of the trees (when he wasn't throwing up) and he had won the lady over. He came back up the pathway beaming from ear to ear.

'She's invited me for tea on Sunday,' he said happily as we took off back up the street and turned into the main road. 'She's my fifth today.'

'Fifth what?'

'New friend. How about you? How many did you make?'

I joined my index finger to my thumb to make a zero. I didn't count Callum Hesketh. I reckoned he wasn't serious. As Ruby had said, he was probably just making a list of new girls to conquer. 'I made at least one enemy though, maybe more.'

Dylan looked genuinely concerned. 'Really?'

'Yep. Welcome to Loserville. Population: me. I am now officially the most unpopular girl in the school.'

'India, tomorrow's another day. You have to pick yourself up, dust yourself off and start all over again,' he said, quoting a song that Mum sings sometimes.

'Dylan . . .'

'Yeah.'

I put my middle finger up to him in a rude gesture by way of reply. Of course it had to be exactly at the moment that Mrs Goldman happened to drive by and glance out from the window of the car. She gave me a *very* disapproving look.

'Oh for puke's sake, can this day *get* any worse?' I groaned as the car drove on.

It could. And it did. Joe came cycling past, saw us, stopped his bike and waited for us to catch him up.

'I . . . oh . . . Hi,' I said with a smile, although I wasn't totally sure of how I felt about him after finding out that he had a girlfriend.

He didn't smile back. 'India, can I have a word?

I immediately felt myself tense up. 'Yeah. Sure.'

Dylan walked on a few steps then he turned around and, behind Joe's back, he clutched his heart and pursed his lips into a kiss expression. I'd strangle him when I got him home.

'What on earth did you say to Mia?' Joe asked when Dylan was out of earshot.

Oh God, I thought. *What has she told him?* 'Nothing. Least . . . Why?'

'She came to find me at lunch break and gave me a right earful. Did you say something to her about us?'

I felt myself go red and I wished that the ground would open

44

up and swallow me. 'No . . . Well, yes, but not really . . . No . . . What is there to say?'

Joe sighed, then raked through his brown hair with his right hand. 'So what's she on about then?'

'I . . . I, er . . . I recognised one of your drawings on the wall. You know, the one above the sink. I said I knew you and we'd met in Greece . . .' (I wasn't going to say that I'd admitted that I had a crush on him, and prayed that Mia hadn't told him either.) 'That's all.'

Joe sighed. 'She seems to have got it into her head that I *cheated* on her . . .'

'*Cheated* on her? No way. I *never* said that. Why would I?'

'That's what I thought because . . . well, nothing happened with us, did it?'

He was looking at me so earnestly and my stomach did the strange double-flip thing it did whenever I looked into his eyes. He really did have extraordinary eyes, jade green with a circle of navy blue outlining the iris, and long thick curly lashes. I could stare into his eyes all day. It was weird. One part of my mind was saying, *Yes, yes, something did happen, a lot happened, we connected, we fell in love . . . least I did.* Another part was saying, *I'm not sure I haven't got chocolate button smeared all over my face.* Another part was having to hold back from leaning forward and nibbling his bottom lip, and a fourth part admitted, *No, nothing happened.* That was the part that spoke. 'No. Course not. I *think* I'd have remembered.'

A fleeting smile crossed Joe's face and he slightly raised his right eyebrow. 'Yeah. Think I'd have remembered too. OK. Sorry. Guess Mia can get a bit jealous sometimes.'

'I guess,' I said, although I was dying to ask a hundred questions. How long have you been going out with her? Is it love? Is it for real? She said it's on-off. Is it on? Or off? Are you having doubts? Would you like a new girlfriend? How about me? Do you like *meeeeeeee*? Do want a chocolate button? Do you want to go to the park and snog till our faces drop off? But of course, I didn't say anything. I cooled it out instead. I'd said too much to all the wrong people already that day so I just stood there like a lemon. A sad lemon. A lemon that had lost its zing. A lemon that was all squeezed out.

Joe turned to go. 'OK. Good. Sorry,' he said, then rolled his eyes. 'Girls, huh?'

'Huh. Yeah. Girls,' I said, then laughed. 'Er . . . although I am one by the way. A girl that is. Not a huh. Not that I know what a huh is.'

Joe laughed and visibly relaxed. 'I know that. Oh yeah, how was your first day?'

I shrugged my shoulders.

'Someone show you around?'

I shrugged my shoulders again. 'Mmf.' I wasn't sure if I wanted to have a cosy little chat with him about my first day, although I was dying to tell someone how truly awful it had been. But if I opened up to Joe, I'd start feeling close to him again, like I had on the plane back from Greece, when we had shared a lot – and I *hadn't* imagined it. But that was before I knew about 'the girlfriend', so I reminded myself he was taken, a no-go area. Mia's, not mine.

I was so relieved to get home ten minutes later and I ran straight upstairs before the inquisition started. Luckily Aunt Sarah wasn't around, nor was Kate, and Dylan was in such good spirits having had the 'best day of his life' that he was straight into the kitchen to tell Mum all about it. I was pleased that he was OK and glad that he would distract Mum from probing me about my day and I could go and get use of the computer first. There was only one person that I wanted to talk to and that was Erin. Luckily, she was already on MSN waiting for me.

Irishbrat4eva:	Where've u been?
Cinnamongirl:	Detention, remember?
Irishbrat4eva:	Oh yeah. How was day one at the loonie bin?
Cinnamongirl:	Woe, woe and thrice times woe.
Irishbrat4eva:	Hah! One day at a school in London and you've come over all merry ole England. OK. Fine. What Shakespeare are you doing?
Cinnamongirl:	Romeo and Jules. You?
Irishbrat4eva:	Now is the winter of our discontent.
Cinnamongirl:	Yeah, I guess it is getting colder.
Irishbrat4eva:	No, idiot. Now is the winter of our discontent – it's a line from the play we're doing – Richard 3rd.
Cinnamongirl:	Whatever, so it's cold outside and tough times are ahead. Get over it, Richard.

Irishbrat4eva: OK so from now on, we must talk in Shakespearian. Oh yay and a hey nonnie no.

Cinnamongirl: Oh yay indeed, but forsooth, for my heart doth lie heavy in mine chest this night and verily, my day has been blackened by the darkest cloud, for never was a story of more pain than that of Joe and his India Jane.

Irishbrat4eva: Alas, poor maiden, bare thy ailing heart to me and tell me of thy suffering.

Cinnamongirl: I am in disgrace in my fellow maidens' eyes and I do beweep alone in my outcast state . . .

Irishbrat4eva: Oh fie and folly . . . poor thee. Beweep? Isn't that what budgies doest? Beweep. Beweep.

I couldn't keep up the typing fast enough. There was too much to tell her so I picked up the phone and filled her in on the real reason I was late for school (it was OK to tell her about Dylan) and about being seen by my Head of Year for giving Dylan the finger.

Erin laughed her head off. 'Excellent! *Totally* top first day. You get a prize. But what was that about lover boy? Did you see him?'

And so I told her about Joe seeing me when I was on my knees in the mud in the rain, about the art class and him having a girlfriend, about Mia and Leela all looking at me with hate in the canteen and lastly, about seeing Joe on the way home.

'He what? He *what*? I am flabbergasted. My gast has never been so flabbered in fact. Are you *kidding*? He has a girlfriend?'

'No, I am not kidding. And yes, he has a girlfriend, but she did say it had been kind of on-off . . .'

'On-off, off-on. Who cares! When was he going to tell you this rather important bit of information? I mean a *whole* summer together and he never mentioned it to you? The rat. The user —'

'No. You've got him wrong. Joe so isn't a rat type.'

'Ah listen to yourself, India Jane. Come on. Wake up and smell the droppings. OK. So. How can you tell the difference between a rat and a nice guy?'

'Is this a joke? I don't know. How can you?'

'You can't. They both look the same. Don't you get it?'

'No. It wasn't like that. And it wasn't a whole summer together. We only saw each other now and then and no way was I going to do the inquisition and scare him off. You know how boys hate that.'

'Yeah, but you had enough conversations and you sat together *all* the way on the plane coming back. Somewhere in the conversation about star signs, what music you like, family info, etc, etc, he might have just mentioned the one tiny fact that he already had a fricking GIRLFRIEND!'

I was starting to feel annoyed with Erin and defensive of Joe and myself. 'Why should he? I mean, he didn't owe me anything . . .'

'He's been leading you on. Having a little flirt. Wanting the best of both worlds. You are being *far* too nice, India Jane. The guy is clearly not worth the ground you walk on. I have changed my mind about him and forbid you to have anything more to do with him.'

'Bossy-boots. Scott Malone was clearly a rat and did I tell you to dump him? No.'

I was starting to feel confused. I hadn't even told her about meeting Callum and suddenly I didn't want to. How had the conversation escalated into an argument with my *best* friend and me feeling like it was me and Joe against her? She was supposed to be on my side . . . She *was* on my side and *that* was why she was angry with Joe. She was being protective. I was relieved when, a moment later, I heard the African gong at the bottom of the stairs that Mum and Aunt Sarah use to announce that supper is ready. (The house is so big that it's the best way.) 'Got to go, Erin. Supper. Speak tomorrow, same time?'

'Oh bollards, now you're mad with me.'

'No I'm not.'

'You are so. I can tell. Your voice has gone all clipped like it does when you're cross.'

'No. I'm fine. Speak tomorrow, same time, and give my love to everyone in my old class. Tell them I miss them all.'

'Sure,' she said. 'But I want you to know that I'm fuming. Smoke is pouring out my ears. One of us has to be mad with Joe.'

'I wasn't his girlfriend, Erin, nor was I his confidante. He wasn't duty bound to tell me anything.'

'Grrrrrrrr. He's been leading you on though with his smouldering looks and he did the magnet-eye thing with you *three* times you said.'

I didn't want to be reminded. I wanted to forget Joe. And Mia. And all of it. 'Got to go. Byeee,' I said as the gong sounded a second time. I put down the phone. I felt bad after talking to her. Why was I defending Joe so much? She was only voicing everything that I had thought myself when I found out that he had a girlfriend. And it was true, we *had* done the magnet-eye thing – that's Erin's expression for when a boy looks at you and it's as if you can't drag your eyes away from looking at each other. It is also usually accompanied by stomach butterflies. But we hadn't snogged or made any promises. *So what now?* I asked myself as I slid down the banisters. *Spaghetti bol, by the smell of the garlic,* said a voice in my head. *I'm starving.*

Supper was like being in a busy café as people came and went during the meal. My brother Lewis (he's a student and has digs with a mate up in Crouch End) popped in with the excuse that he'd come to see how my and Dylan's first day went. We didn't buy it. We knew he'd come because he wanted a decent meal. He had also brought Mum a pile of his dirty washing to do (lucky Mum). Mum doesn't mind the meal bit because she knows he lives on takeaways in the flat, but she thinks he's got a cheek that she is still expected to wash his clothes! Not that she refuses. She's too soft by half, I think, although she did nag him to get his hair cut. It's on his shoulders, but I think the scruffy-rock-star look suits him. Kate wafted in halfway through supper, turned her nose up at the spaghetti bol and made herself some cheese on toast instead. When she asked how our day had gone, I lied through my teeth and said it had been brilliant, and Dylan told the truth, except about the throwing up on the way there. Dylan and I caught each other's eye at one point and he winked at me. I wasn't going to tell anyone about the puke episode and he wasn't going to reveal that I hadn't made any friends. Just as we were finishing, Ethan (my stepbrother from Dad's first marriage), Jess (his wife) and their twins, Eleanor and Lara, arrived. They're gorgeous girls with dark curly hair like their dad's (and grandad's), big blue eyes and very cheeky faces. Jess stands out as the only blonde English rose amongst all of us with Italian blood. The twins dived straight under the table and thought it highly amusing to pretend to be dogs and bite people's ankles when they were eating. I didn't mind. It took my mind off my horrible day, and by the time supper was over, I was feeling a whole lot better (apart from the tiny teeth marks). And as if he'd picked up on the fact that all the family was there, Dad called and, of course, the phone had to handed around to everyone, including the twins under the table, so that he didn't feel left out.

I sent Erin a message later that evening. I knew that I wouldn't be able to sleep if she was upset with me along with the rest of the world.

Cinnamongirl: Forsooth, but my repast dost lie heavy in mine stomach, for verily I have stuffed myself like a boar at a Mayflower Ball.

She was still online, as if she had been waiting for me.

Irishbrat4eva: Verily, sweet maid, sometimes it is the season for stuffing thy face so waste not thy time in vain regret. And forgive this ignorant peasant forthwith and hence forth because I do shooteth my mouth off sometimes, but tis because thou art my mate and it doth smote me heavily to see thy heart lie wounded and cast aside like a . . . cast aside thing. Verily I do not wish you to cast thy pearls before swines.

Cinnamongirl: Fear not, O princess of the green land, for tomorrow be a new day with a new lark or is it a nightingale? (And round here you couldst throw in a car alarm too).

Irishbrat4eva: That's the attitude. Sweet dreams, O princess of the red, white and blue land.

Cinnamongirl: Ah yes to sleep, to dream of better boys to come. And so, weary with my toil, I haste me to my bed, fare thee well my one and only true friend, etc, etc.

Irishbrat4eva: Verily verily, yeah, etc, etc. Zzzzzzzzzzzzzzzzzz.

Chapter 5

Sorry, Sorry, Sorry

The next day, Dylan and I were at school on time, no throwing up on the way and no major disasters. *It's going to be OK*, I told myself as we went to class after assembly. *I can start over. Make it work here.*

First lesson was double maths, my least favourite subject and my teacher was a strict-looking skinny lady with a scrawny neck and wiry grey hair. She was called Mrs Hunt and she had that puckering around her mouth that people who've smoked all their life sometimes have. I guess it comes from the repetition of sucking in a thousand cigarettes. *Eau de la Fag Ash by Mal B'Orough – she's definitely a smoker*, I thought as she wafted by and I caught the faint smell of stale tobacco.

I was lucky in class in that I had managed to get a desk on the back row from where I could watch everyone. I still got a few stares as the new girl, but people settled in and soon got on with work, except for one dark-haired boy who I remembered from yesterday's register as being called Mikey. He kept turning round and grinning at me. I smiled back in a friendly way, but then he kept doing it and I wondered if I'd got a smudge on my face or something. Although he had a sweet face, he wasn't fanciable – too chubby in a way that made him look like a fifteen-year-old toddler. None of the boys in my year were boyfriend material. They all looked too young; in fact, a couple of them were tiny, about a foot smaller than I was, and looked more like Year Eights than Year Elevens, whereas some of the girls looked like they could easily pass for eighteen or older.

From my vantage point, Leela seemed to be mates with two girls. One was called Brook. I'd been behind her in the morning's assembly. I'd noticed her because of her hair – it was fab, dark and straight and cut at a sleek angle from the back to the jaw so that it was longer at the front. It looked really cool. The other was the girl I'd seen with Leela in the hall yesterday, who was called Zahrah. I could tell that they'd been talking about me because they'd fallen silent when I'd walked in and started staring at the ceiling as if there was something really interesting up there. I said hi as I made my way to the back. I had nothing to be ashamed of. I wasn't a boyfriend stealer.

As Mrs Hunt went through some equations on the board, I took advantage of my position at the back to check out my classmates further. Nicole and Ruby were on my left at the back and were clearly thick as thieves. *Definitely a pair of princesses, but they might be fun as mates*, I thought, *but probably wouldn't want a threesome.* Leela and her two looked like a laugh, but so far, I was in their bad books. There was a bunch of geeky boys at the front. A couple of cute boys near the back who were trying to act cool and would probably be hits with the younger girls, but if they stood up, they would only come up to my shoulders. A serious-looking girl with dark hair pulled back and cool Italian black-framed glasses. A girl with ginger hair. A couple of Muslim girls in their hijabs on the left. A tall girl with brown hair, who was very pretty and had managed to get away with wearing black kohl around her eyes. A pretty black girl with her hair in braids. Nobody out of the ordinary, except maybe Ruby who had the X-factor. They were just teenagers. Most of the girls had long hair tied back. They looked OK. No daughters of Satan lurking behind their fringes. No weirdoes, least not on first glance. *Which of you will be my friend, or my friends?* I asked myself as I stared at the back of their heads. *Who would I like to hang out with? Phone after school to mull over the day with? Spend my weekends with? Share my secrets with? What do I even want from a friend? Why is Erin my friend? Because she's a laugh but she also talks sense when needed and —*

'India Jane, India *Jane*! Are you paying attention?' barked Mrs Hunt from the front.

'Yes, Miss.'

'So? What is the answer?'

I had no idea what she was talking about.

'Er . . . ynuf . . .' I blustered.

'*Not* a good start, India Jane,' Mrs Hunt huffed. 'You have a lot of ground to cover in order to catch up and daydreaming is not the way to do it.'

Tell me about it, I thought as everyone swivelled around to watch me turn bright pink.

In the break, I left my portfolio with Mr Bailey and then I went looking for Mia. I couldn't see her in the hall or the canteen, but just before the bell went for the next class, I saw her coming out of the girls' cloakroom.

'Mia,' I called.

She glanced back, and as soon as she saw me, her expression clouded. I was clearly the last person she wanted to talk to, but I wasn't going to be put off.

'I really need to speak to you about Joe,' I said.

She held up her hand as if to halt me and shook her head. 'I don't want to hear wha—'

'No. You *have* to listen,' I persisted. 'Joe didn't cheat on you. Yes, I fancied him, but you *knew* that anyhow because I told you I had a crush on someone, but *he* doesn't know how I feel. Really. Nothing happened with us. Honest. You *can* trust me. I'm not the type of person who would steal someone else's boyfriend. I'm really not but I didn't know . . .'

Mia's lip tightened. 'Exactly. You didn't know about me. He didn't tell you. And why do you think that was?'

I shrugged. 'I don't know, but we didn't spend that much time together. Really, we didn't. He was working down in the village most days so I can count the times that we spoke on one hand.'

And repeat every line of dialogue because it's imprinted on my brain, I thought. 'Don't feel bad because of me, that's all I wanted to say. Joe didn't cheat on you with me or anyone else in Greece.'

Mia's face softened. 'Actually Joe told me that nothing happened with you so I guess I overreacted a bit. Just . . . well, Joe Donahue had a reputation as player before we got together, everyone fancied him and in the beginning I never knew where I was with him, so . . . I jumped to conclusions and assumed he'd gone back to being the school Casanova. Boys, huh?'

I had to smile as Joe had almost said the same thing yesterday when he'd said, 'Girls, huh?'

'Well, you can trust me,' I said.

Mia smiled back. 'OK. And I am sorry. I guess you didn't need all that, it being your first day as well.'

I nodded. 'It's day two now though. Life goes on.'

'Exactly,' said Mia. 'Good for you.'

'Get to class, girls,' called Mrs Goldman from the end of the corridor. 'The bell's already gone.'

I set off for double French feeling a lot more positive. I was sure that Mia would fill Leela and her friends in and then maybe they'd come round to letting me hang out with them sometimes.

French was a breeze as I'm good at languages, although by the end of the morning I had an almighty great headache. There were some pupils from the maths class plus about ten I hadn't seen before. As in maths, I glanced them over and they checked me out. *I guess it's to be expected*, I thought as I tried to greet their stares with a friendly expression.

When the bell went for lunch, I made a dash for outside and fresh air. As I headed out towards the playground, I bumped into Mr Bailey who was coming the opposite way.

'Ah, India,' he said when he spotted me. 'I've looked over your portfolio and I have to say I was most impressed, especially by your landscapes – you have a great sense of colour and perspective. I was so impressed, in fact, I'd like you to take over the scenery-painting. Think you can do it?'

'Nu—' I started.

'Excellent. That's settled then.'

'No. I mean, *no* as in I don't think I can do it. I've never done anything like that before and I'm new here and —'

'It will be a great way for you to meet people then, get involved – and there's no time like the present. You'll be fine. You can obviously draw. And there will be others who have done it before, know the ropes, and can advise. We can't have the same people being in charge every year, can we? Andrea Ward from Year Twelve has done it for the last two years so it's time for a change. Yes. New blood. The job's yours. No big hurry for your side of things as long as you have an idea for . . . oh say, after half-term. In the meantime, we'll be cracking on with the casting and so on. Come to the first meeting a week on Saturday, get to know everyone on your team, meet the director, etc, etc. Introduce yourself to everyone. Plenty of time – but it would be good to get thinking about it soon. And it will look good on your CV. So that's settled.'

'But sir . . .'

'Excellent, carry on,' he said and he produced a pair of Ray

Ban sunglasses, put them on and burst through the doors to the playground with the air of a rock celebrity about to walk into a wall of paparazzi.

I was going to follow him when I heard someone shout down the corridor. As I listened, my heart began to race. Someone was in trouble. The shout turned to a scream. Not a fun I'm-having-a-laugh-type scream. This sounded like someone in distress. I raced along the corridor and looked inside the room from where it was coming. It was Leela who was screaming! She was crumpled down on her knees side on to me and Zahrah was standing in front of her. Zahrah was hitting her and Leela had her arms up in front of her face in defence. Zahrah lifted her arm and swiped it at Leela, who fell back with a cry.

I ran in, grabbed Zahrah's arm and wrenched her away with all my strength. 'Hey! Get off her!'

Zahrah swivelled around in surprise. 'What?'

'You heard me,' I said as I pinned her arms behind her back then did the special knee lock that I had done a few days earlier on Dylan. Zahrah folded into a heap in front of me.

'What the hell? What do you think you're doing?' she cried.

'Getting you off Leela, you bully. I don't care what she's done but you *never* hit a mate!' I said, then turned to Leela. 'You OK Leela?' I reached over to help her up.

Leela looked in a state of total shock. 'No, India!' she said as she sat up. 'What . . .'

It was at that moment I realised that Zahrah and Leela weren't the only people in the room. Oh no. Seated at the back of the room were about a *dozen* students and a young female teacher.

'Wha . . . what on earth are you doing?' Leela spluttered.

Some of the students had their mouths open in surprise. Others were laughing. One of the students even began to clap. I felt totally bewildered and felt my cheeks burn red.

The teacher stepped forward. 'It's OK,' she said then she turned to the class. 'Hush. *Hush.*' Then she turned back to me. 'What's your name?'

'India Jane.'

'India Jane,' she said then added with a slight smile, 'I'm Mrs Maris. Welcome to the lunchtime *drama* group . . .'

Ohwohwoh Gododdoddddddd, I thought as the penny dropped.

'We're rehearsing a scene where indeed Leela's character does get bullied by Zahrah's,' continued Mrs Maris, 'so well done, girls. Well played. Very convincing. You managed to fool a fellow pupil. In today's lesson, India Jane, we are practising techniques for stage fighting. Would you like demonstrate again, girls?'

Zahrah didn't look too happy and threw me a filthy look as she scrambled to her feet, then she and Leela went into an impressive fake fight routine. Zahrah positioned herself so that she had her back to us, so that when she raised her arm and slapped down, we couldn't see her actually touch Leela. The moment her arm came down, Leela shrieked and fell back as if she'd been struck.

'It's all about positioning, timing and the reaction of the person being hit,' said the teacher. 'Next time you see a fight on

TV, everyone, you'll notice how it's done. No one ever touches anyone else, it just looks as though they do, and you'll often find that the person doing the punching or slapping has their back to the camera so that you only see the reaction of the so-called victim. Once more, girls.'

I stepped to the side so that I had a better view of the oncoming slap. It was clear. When Zahrah went to slap Leela, she stopped about five centimetres short of her face, but Leela yelped as if she'd really been hit and fell back as if she had been struck hard. And then they went into a realistic hair-pulling sequence with Leela's hand on top of Zahrah's hand on Leela's head and much squealing from Leela.

'See, it looks authentic,' said Mrs Maris, 'but actually Zahrah isn't pulling at all. See. It is actually Leela who is in control there, but to the audience, it looks like it is Zahrah.'

Dylan will love this, I thought as in my mind's eye I saw us fake fighting and freaking Mum out, but my fantasy didn't last long. Zahrah was looking at me disdainfully.

'I'm so sorry,' I said and began to back out of the room. 'I thought that Lee . . . well, you know what I thought . . .'

'I think it's commendable that you came to her rescue,' said Mrs Maris. 'Some people would pretend that they hadn't heard or would not have wanted to get involved, so good for you, India Jane.'

One of the pupils put up her hand to ask a question and Mrs Maris went over to her.

Zahrah came over to me. 'And other people would have

known immediately that I am *not* a bully,' she said. 'I find it insulting that you actually thought me capable of hurting anyone – especially Leela. She's my mate.'

'I'm really, really sorry,' I said. I felt foolish and upset that I might have offended Zahrah. I wanted to get away. It must have shown on my face because when I turned to leave, Leela looked at me kindly, smiled and mock-strangled herself. It was exactly the sort of mad thing that Erin would have done and made me realise just how much I was missing her.

I made a swift exit and was heading for the cloakroom when someone behind tapped me on the shoulder. I turned to see an earnest-looking girl with shoulder-length wavy ginger hair. She looked at me coldly. 'India Jane?'

I nodded.

'I saw you talking to Mr Bailey before.'

I nodded again.

'I'm Andrea —'

'Ward,' I finished for her. 'Oh yes. Mr Bailey said that you'd done the scenery so far and —'

'Yeah. I have. Two years running. I'm going to study it at college, which is why I don't appreciate newcomers waltzing in and taking my role. That's my thing and I was really looking forward to designing the scenery. *The Boy Friend* was *my* choice of show, did Bailey tell you that? And now I can't believe I won't get to do the sets. I had so many ideas.'

'I didn't want to do it. I *don't* want to do it. It was all Mr Bailey's idea. Please, you can do it, you really can. I don't even

63

know the story of *The Boy Friend*. He said we could work together.'

'No way. I'm not taking orders from someone in Year Eleven. Especially someone who's never done it before.'

'I'll do what you want. Really I will,' I insisted. 'Especially as you already have ideas of what to do. That's great.'

'*Was* great, but Mr Bailey said I have to step aside and give someone else a chance. He knows what my ideas were and he's not going to like it if I make you do them, is he?'

'I am so sorry,' I said.

'Easy to say, isn't it?' she said as she turned on her heel and walked off. 'You've ruined everything.'

What a totally excellent morning. Not, I thought as I headed back up to the school library, where I intended to hide for the rest of the lunch break. *So much for starting over, I thought. Today's been even worse than yesterday and it's not even over yet! I might get one of those advertising sandwich boards that people wear over their shoulders. The front could say,* New girl, No mates *and the back could say,* Sorry, sorry, sorry.

Chapter 6

Friends Wanted – Apply Here

'So what exactly do you want?' asked Lewis on the Sunday after my first week, when we'd been talking about my role as a Molly No Mates over lunch.

I handed him the tub of mango ice cream from the freezer and he doled it out into four bowls. 'Not a lot. Someone to hang out with.'

Mum frowned. 'Hmmm. Think you'll find you want more than that, India.'

'Yeah,' said Lewis. 'It's like with relationships with girls. I want more than just someone to hang out with.'

'So what do you want then?' I asked.

'A supermodel with enormous knockers who has a degree in quantum physics, cooks like a celebrity chef and adores me.'

'Yeah. Me too,' said Dylan.

Mum rolled her eyes up to the ceiling. 'Lord, what have I raised?' she asked herself.

'Got to aim high, India Jane,' said Lewis. 'You know the saying, if you aim for the top of the tree, you'll get to the lower branches . . .'

'If you aim for the stars, you'll reach the top of the tree,' I said. I knew the quote well as it was one of Dad's favourites.

'Make a list,' said Mum. 'It's always good to be clear about what you want. Friendships that you make when you're a teenager can last you a lifetime. They're very important – your friends can be there through all the highs and lows that life can bring.' She got up and handed me a piece of paper. 'Come on. Write down what you want in a friend.'

'I don't know, Mum. What did you ever want in a friend?'

Mum looked thoughtful for a few moments. 'Someone who lets me be myself. Actually your dad is my best friend, which is why I miss him so much. With all the travelling, I never really developed lasting friends outside of the family. I always had you lot to occupy my time, and then there was Sarah here if ever I wanted a girl to talk to . . . but she's always out, on business. In fact, like you, India, I really need to make some new friends of my own.'

It hadn't occurred to me that Mum might be lonely as she was always so cheerful but listening to her made me realise, of course, that she was missing Dad like I was missing Erin.

I stared at the paper. *Someone who* . . . I started to write. I didn't get any further as the doorbell went and Ethan burst in with a twin under either arm. He looked red and flustered and like he hadn't slept for a week.

'I have to go to the supermarket and I'm not taking these two again, so please can you babysit? Anyone?'

'Why don't you want to take them with you?' asked Dylan as Ethan set the girls down on the floor.

Ethan snorted. 'Last time I took them shopping, they started auditioning for roles in *The Exorcist* – Eleanor puked over the organic veg and Lara started screaming the place down. They totally freaked out some of the customers. No. When we're out, we are officially the family that everyone wants to get away from. Please, anyone . . . ?'

'I've got homework,' said Dylan.

'I'm too irresponsible,' said Lewis.

'Put the girls in the fridge,' sniggered Dylan. 'We can have twin popsicles later.'

'Or we could boil them,' said Lewis. 'Twin brain is a delicacy in some countries, you know.'

Eleanor and Lara squealed and hid behind Ethan's legs.

Mum rolled her eyes. 'Honestly, why do you start acting like twelve-year-olds when you get together?'

'Because I *am* twelve,' said Dylan.

'And I'm emotionally retarded,' said Lewis.

Ethan looked pleadingly at me. 'I'll give you a fiver,' he said.

'Done,' I said. Art could wait.

And that was the end of my friendship list and my afternoon.

★ ★ ★

The following week flew by and I found that catching up on my schoolwork was taking up the majority of my time and focus. Despite my best efforts in the time that was left, the friendship situation was still in crisis – apart from Mikey, who I'd discovered lived in the next street from me. Some mornings or evenings, he'd catch up with Dylan and me and walk into school with us. On Friday, he saw that I was looking down as we filed out of the school gates and he offered to buy me a hot chocolate in the local Starbucks.

'So tell Uncle Mikey all,' he said after we'd got our drinks and bagged the sofa on the left of the café.

'I'm not going to snog you,' I said. 'So you can drop the agony aunt routine.'

Mikey did a face of surprise horror. '*Moi?* Think I'd try that stunt on a bright girl like you?'

'Yeah. I have brothers, you know. I know what kind of tricks boys can get up to.'

Mikey laughed. 'OK, OK, but seriously, how's your week been? I am interested. *Really.* You were saying before – hard to find friends?'

'Yeah. It's not for lack of trying,' I said.

'You need to do an activity where you can get to know people naturally,' he suggested as he took a sip of his drink and, without realising, gave himself a chocolate moustache.

'Like what?' I asked.

'Chess or ice-skating,' he replied and then noticed me looking at the chocolate on his lip. 'What?'

'Chocolate all over your lip,' I said.

He stuck out his tongue and licked the chocolate off, then wiped his lip with the back of his hand.

I pulled a face. 'Hmm. Remind me to eat out in public with you again.'

Mikey shrugged and grinned. 'So? Chess or ice-skating?'

'I'm crap at both. I get my knights mixed up with my bishops, and the only time I ever tried ice-skating I fell flat on my bum after five minutes and have had a recurring nightmare ever since that, while flat on my back, someone skates over my fingers and slices them off. Freaky.'

'OK. So what else? Try after-school activities, that's a great way to meet people.'

'I tried hockey on Wednesday. The hockey club were looking for new players for the team. I missed a number of balls then hit a cracker into the captain's right leg. Needless to say, I wasn't picked.'

Mikey grimaced. 'Early days.'

'I guess. I did meet someone on the way to school on Monday. You'd gone in already. Grace. She dropped her travelcard and I picked it up and ran after her. I thought that we might be mates until we got to the school gates, where another girl was waiting for her. She gave me a filthy look, linked arms with Grace and hauled her off. Like, two's company, three's a crowd.'

'Girls can be like that. Anybody else?'

'In media studies, I was partnered with a girl called Holly. She was great, really chatty, but I soon realised that if I spent more than half an hour with her, I'd have to kill her. She was fun but had the LOUDEST voice. And no attention span. Like I'd be telling her something and she'd be looking over my shoulder, clearly not listening.'

Mikey looked over my shoulder. 'Sorry, what were you saying?' he said. 'Only joking. I was listening. Sounds like you've had a crap week . . . Oh God, there's more?'

I nodded. 'You *did* ask. I met someone in maths. We hung out for a couple break times together. She was nice until a boy appeared – any boy – and then she'd turn her back on me and start acting really weird, like Miss Cutie Cue, twirling her hair in her fingers and pouting and talking in a little girlie lispy voice that made me want to slap her.'

'Poor you. Er . . . what was her name?'

'Mikey! Don't tell me you fall for that girlie-girl act?'

'Me? No? Course not . . . Er, OK. What class is she in?'

I gave him a light pinch on his upper arm. At that moment, Chloe Fitzgerald from our class waved at us from the queue at the counter.

'There. She looks like she wants to be friends,' said Mikey.

'Maybe, she was really nice to me yesterday lunchtime, but it came out that she'd been talking to someone who had been talking to my cousin Kate and had found out that my dad was a count. She already knew that Kate's mum was Sarah Rosen —'

'Of the über-trendy shops?'

I nodded. 'I soon realised that she didn't want me as a mate,

70

she wanted to get in with my family.'

'Chloe can be a bit like that. Bit of a social climber. Always wanting to get in with whoever she thinks might be somebody.'

'I should have told her that although my dad has a title, his family hasn't had any money for years because some ancient relative gambled it away and we're totally cash poor. It's only my aunt who has the dosh.'

'That's why I want to hang out with you,' said Mikey. 'I am really after your aunt, as I like older women and they like me and my boyish charm, don't you know.'

'Yeah. Aunt Sarah really goes for guys who get chocolate moustaches on their upper lips when they're out. Mikey, be serious. My life is in crisis.'

Mikey made his expression go serious and he looked over at me as if I'd told him I had an hour to live. It made me laugh. Chloe was joined at the counter by another girl I'd met during the week. I nudged Mikey. 'Do you know her?'

He nodded. 'Ella. No sense of humour.'

'Tell me about it. Sense of humour is high on my list of friendship requirements.'

'Mine too. That and enormous knockers.'

I rolled my eyes. 'You sound like my stupid brothers.'

'I'll take that as a compliment.'

'What about Nicole and Ruby in our class?' I asked. 'They look like fun.'

Mikey pulled a face. 'You could do better,' he said. 'They're a pair of spoiled princesses.'

I smiled. *Out of your league*, I thought, but I didn't say it. It felt good to be sitting in the café having a gossip with him, and I began to realise that I wasn't as alone as I'd thought I was. I had the beginning of a friendship with him. If only he wasn't being so nice in the hope that I'd go out with him, because that was never going to happen. As we were chatting, I decided that, from then on, I wasn't going to try so hard to find friends. I was going to relax and be cooler about it.

'See that girl behind Ella?' he said as he pointed to a tall dark-haired girl in the queue. 'She's a right bossy git. She will probably be go on to be prime minister then go for world dominance.'

'One of those larger-than-life people? Unlike me. I've had a small day today.'

'Small day?'

I nodded. 'Yeah. Like Alice in Wonderland. Remember in the book, she drank a potion and grew and grew until she was bursting out of the house, she was so big. And then she drank another potion and shrank until she was tiny, as small as a mouse. Some days, I feel big and confident, other days, I feel like shrinking away and want to avoid everyone. Today's one of my small days and I feel like giving up.' Suddenly I had an idea. 'Hey, Mikey. Will you take some pics of me?'

'Naked?'

'*No.* I've had an idea for my self-portrait project.'

'I am your slave, India Jane. I will do whatever you ask me and one day you will realise that I am your soul mate, your lover, your man.'

'OK, but first you need to grow about four inches.'

'I'm working on it.'

I could see the pictures in my mind's eye. In one, I'd be tiny; in another, enormous. I was sure that with a bit of tinkering, the right background and props, I could make the pictures work. I would call them 'Alice in Wonderland Days'.

'Mikey.'

'Yeah.'

'I think we can be friends.'

'It's a start. So, I suppose a snog is out of the question?'

'You suppose right.'

Mikey nodded and smiled. 'I have time on my side . . . but meanwhile, if you're not interested, maybe you could give me some tips for pulling girls. See there's this girl in French I fancy . . .'

Mikey was cool. OK, so maybe I'd have preferred a girl mate, but he was a good start.

On the way home, I began to wonder if my expectations for a friend were too high. I waited until our agreed MSN time, then I asked Erin what she thought.

Cinnamongirl: Forsooth my friend in the green country, dost I ask too much of a fellow traveller on the road of life? Amst I being too picky?

Irishbrat4eva: Nay, fair maiden in the red, white and blue. Fie on thy dark thoughts, banish them from thy mind.

	Thou asks for nowt that thou canst not give thyself. And tis understandable that thou would wanst someone likst me, but I'm a one off. Irreplaceable. A super-friend.
Cinnamongirl:	Modest too.
Irishbrat4eva:	Indeed. Modesty is another of my many attributes. Have thou seenst the dark prince? How goes it with Donahue the Dubious?
Cinnamongirl:	Forsooth, our paths cross not. I see him from afar from places whence I do not go, as he is of the Elders and I am below him in years.
Irishbrat4eva:	Grieve not. Tis his loss not thine.
Cinnamongirl:	Verily and henceforth, when it comes to friends and boys, I shall be the flower, not the busy bee. I shall letteth them come to me and not put out this vibe of Needy Noodles of Notting Hill.
Irishbrat4eva:	Verily. Desperate Doras never did winneth friend nor foe, hey nonny.

When we'd finished our catch up, I realised once again, Erin was my perfect friend. She had just one small fault. She lived in another blooming country.

Chapter 7

Meeting, Schmeeting

Oh whoa whoa nooo, I thought when I saw who was waiting in the prefab where the show meeting was to be held. Medium frame, broad shoulders, slim waist, cute butt. In jeans and a black T-shirt. Shoulder-length brown hair. Gorgeous eyes. Joe.

I took a deep breath as my stomach did its usual lurch. 'Hey.'

He turned and smiled. 'Hey, India. How you getting on?'

'Good. Yeah. What are you doing in here?'

'Scenery-painting. I do it most years. You?'

'Scenery-painting. First year.'

'Ah. Good. Should be an interesting one.'

'Oh. Why's that?'

'Andrea Ward told me that some dork with no ideas at all has been put in charge.'

'She did. Really? Er . . . I . . .'

At that moment, the door opened and a couple of other people sauntered in and Joe waved hi to them and went over to chat. After a few more minutes, Mr Bailey appeared with Mrs Maris and a couple of other teachers I recognised from the drama department. After fifteen minutes, there were about forty of us.

Mr Bailey got up on to a table and clapped his hands. 'Right everybody, you all know why we're here. We won't waste any time as we want to get on. For anyone who doesn't know the director of this year's show, I'd like to introduce Barry Morrison. Say hi, Barry.' He looked down at a tall dark-haired boy with a long pale face who was standing by the table. He barely looked up, but gave the gathered pupils a weary wave. *Attractive in a goth poet kind of way*, I thought. *He looks interesting.*

'Get yourself into your groups,' Mr Bailey continued, 'I've spoken to you all so you know where you belong. Actors, top right – see Mrs Maris. Technical, glad to see some of you showed up, very good, just have a quick chat then you can go. Scenery, back right by the door. Costumes and make-up, back left. Right, chop, chop.' He attempted a balletic leap to the floor and almost lost his balance when he landed. He glanced quickly at the other teachers to see if they'd noticed his momentary lapse in cool, but they weren't taking any notice of him.

I made my way to the back, where he'd indicated the scenery group should go. I glanced around, but there was no sign of Andrea in the hall. I got out a couple of sketchpads and tried to look busy as I waited for the others and was soon joined by Joe, two other boys and three girls.

'So where's Andrea?' asked a boy with spiky red hair and freckles.

'She'll be along later,' said a skinny blonde girl with a brace. 'She's still upset that she's been usurped.'

'So where is our new leader then?' asked Joe.

The freckly boy shrugged. 'Anyone know if it's a girl or boy?'

'Girl,' said the blonde.

'And Andrea said she seemed like a bit of moron,' Joe added, 'and it's going to be up to us to pull toge—' He glanced over at me, including me in what he was saying, but as soon as he saw my face, he put two and two together and sat down and slapped his forehead with the palm of his hand. 'Yeah. Um. Hah! Think I'll sit down for a moment.' And then he looked as if he was having a hard time not laughing.

I stood up. 'I guess I'd better introduce myself. I'm India Jane Ruspoli. I'm the moron who's been put in charge.'

Joe couldn't contain himself and burst out laughing. 'Sorry, India. *Really* sorry. Sorry for laughing. I should have guessed.'

Everyone else looked bewildered, like they didn't know how to play it, and looked from me to Joe to me again.

'She's not a moron, guys,' said Joe. 'I know her. At least kind of . . . kind of know her, that is. Not that she's a kind of moron either. Whatever . . .' I felt touched that Joe had come to my defence and for once, it was my turn to be amused as he blustered over what he was trying to say. 'Main thing is, she can really paint.'

'How do you know?' I asked. I knew that he'd never seen any

of my work, even though he'd asked to see some sketches when we were in Greece.

'I saw your portfolio. It was on the side in the art room and I saw your name on it.'

'That was private!'

Joe coloured slightly. 'I know. Er . . . oops,' he said and pointed at himself. 'Nosey bugger. That's me. I couldn't resist. It would be like finding your diary.'

'My *diary*! You'd read my *diary*?'

The ginger boy coughed. 'Er, excuse me, but others *are* present here.'

'Yeah. Like, get a room,' drawled the blonde girl.

Joe looked taken aback at her comment and not very pleased about it.

'Sorry,' I said. 'Yes. Shall we get on with the meeting?'

'Might be an idea,' said Blondie. 'You two can get back to flirting with each other later . . .'

'We weren't . . .' Joe and I blurted at the same time.

The others exchanged looks, as if sharing a private joke.

'Whatever,' said Blondie. 'Shall we get started?'

'I'm Tim,' said the ginger-haired boy and indicated the plump dark-haired boy next to him. 'This is Mark. We're both in Year Twelve.'

I turned to the girls. 'Ruth,' said the blonde one.

'And Gayle,' said her equally sullen-looking brunette mate.

At that moment, the door opened and in came Andrea. It was a brilliant entrance as, by chance, behind her the sun burst through the clouds at the exact moment she entered the room.

'Wow. Cool lighting effects,' said Tim.

Andrea gave him a smug smile. 'You know me,' she said. 'Andrea's the name. Special effects are the game . . .' And then she saw me. 'Or at least used to be.'

'Yeah,' said Joe. 'How long have you been waiting out there for exactly the right conditions?'

'As if. I have better things to do with my time,' said Andrea, but she flashed him a smile then turned to look at me. 'So. How far have we got?'

'India had just introduced herself,' said Joe with a smirk. 'What was it you said again? Something about a moron?'

I gave him a filthy look and turned my back on him. 'As I was saying . . . Mr Bailey has asked me to co-ordinate the scenery-painting this year but it's my first time so I hope that you'll help me out and tell me when I'm going wrong. Basically, I hope that we can work as a team.'

'We always work as a team,' said Andrea. 'But first we have to have an idea to work on. I presume that you've brought something to show us?'

'Sure,' I said and pulled out my sketchpad. 'I worked on a couple of things last night. But first have any of you got anything to show?'

They shook their heads.

'Andrea, I thought you had something?'

'Yeah, but you go ahead first,' she said with a fake smile.

I passed around my sketches and a couple of interiors that I had cut out of a magazine that showed a nineteen-twenties art deco style. 'I thought we could go for really simple, black-and-white art deco. Seeing as the play is set in a girls' school in the nineteen-twenties, it would seem fitting, don't you think?'

No one looked enthusiastic.

'I suppose that's the problem with coming on board late,' Andrea said. 'We did an art deco set for last year's Christmas show, so if we did it again, it wouldn't look like we'd made much of an effort, would it?'

Bollards, I thought. *So stupid of me. I should have checked what had been done in the past so that I didn't waste my time by going over old ground.*

'Not your fault,' said Joe, coming to my rescue again. 'Bailey should have filled you in when he briefed you.'

Tim and Mark kindly spent the next ten minutes going over past ideas so that I was in the picture. It seemed that, over the years, they'd explored and exhausted a whole host of good ideas: all one colour, sci-fi, nineteen-fifties glamour, medieval . . . the list went on.

'So you got anything else?' Andrea asked me. 'Or has today been a total waste of time?'

'Don't be a bitch,' said Joe. 'This is India's first time on this *and* she's new to the school.'

Andrea narrowed her eyes and scrutinised Joe. 'Not new to you though, I hear. Mia told me that you spent the summer together,' she said.

Joe wasn't intimidated and he stared right back at Andrea until eventually she had to lower her eyes. 'Don't believe everything you hear,' he said. 'We were on the same island, but I wouldn't say we spent the summer together, would you, India?'

'Nothing like,' I said. *Although I would have gladly*, I thought.

'Yeah, let's cut her some slack,' said Mark. 'Look. Let's go through the plot, through the scenes, and see if anyone thinks of anything.'

'I already have,' said Andrea. 'I had it all mapped out in my head.'

'Come on then, let's see your ideas,' said Gayle.

Andrea hesitated, then got out a sketchpad. 'OK,' she said as she produced some sheets. 'I thought we should go gloriously pink. Like OTT romantic and camp.' She passed around some coloured sketches and everyone glanced over them, but no one looked enthusiastic about her ideas either. Although the drawings were good, the sets looked very girlie. 'Well at least I had a new idea.'

'Why don't we chew it over for the rest of the weekend,' suggested Joe. 'And Bailey did say we had until after half-term so it's not like it's urgent.'

'Good idea,' I said, 'and if you have any other suggestions, you can email me or see me at school. And Andrea, I think this is a great idea. Let me talk to the director and see what he thinks.'

'You mean you haven't already?' asked Andrea in an exasperated tone. 'I would have thought that would have been the first thing that you did – you know, find out what direction he wanted to take. Oh for heaven's sake, India, *everybody* knows that the show is the director's baby! It's his vision. I can't *believe* you haven't talked to him!'

Joe shot her a warning glance. 'This is India's first time, remember?'

Andrea shrugged her shoulders. 'OK, OK,' she said and collected her things up and headed towards the door.

Stupid, stupid idiot, I told myself as I gathered my things. *Andrea was dead right. I should have talked to the director. Where the heck has my head been? These guys will think that a moron really has been put in charge.*

There seemed no point in prolonging our part of the meeting and I could see that Barry was still talking to Mrs Maris at the front of the room, so I wrapped things up then made my way out of the hall. Outside, it was a lovely clear day and unseasonably warm for September. The others went and sat on a wall opposite, where Tim got out a packet of Malboro lights and passed them around, but only Gayle took one. I glanced over, wondering whether to go and join them, but I saw Andrea look in my direction then she stood and turned her back on me. Gayle stood and did the same. It was as if they were closing ranks. I got the message: not welcome. I realised that I had left my jacket inside, so went back in to get it, and when I came out, they all seemed deep in conversation. *Probably talking about me and what a disaster I am*, I thought and was about to set off home when Joe glanced up, then came over.

'Don't let Andrea or the others get to you,' he said. 'They're actually all right when things get going and I am sure if you can come up with a good idea, they'll get behind it.'

'I wouldn't count on it,' I said.

'You can count on Tim and Mark. They're not into politics. And I'll do what I can. And speak to Barry. He's the director and a mate of mine.'

'Have you got any idea what he wants?'

'Not really. I saw him a couple of days ago and all he said was he wanted to do something different.'

'That helps a lot. Not. What did you think of the pink theme?'

Joe pulled a face. 'Bit camp for my liking. Let's try and come up with something else, hey?'

'I really need to speak to Barry first I think, he's the director after all,' I said. 'Have you got his number? I could call him later.'

Joe nodded. 'Try him now. I'm sure he'd be cool.' He pulled a mobile out from his pocket, found Barry's number and handed me the phone. A moment later, Barry answered.

'Oh. Hi. I'm India Jane —'

'Scenery, right?'

'Yeah. I . . . er, before we go off in a direction you definitely don't want, have you any idea what you do?'

'Hah! I wish. To tell the truth, I haven't had much time to think about the scenery – too busy with the casting and getting the scripts finalised. Hey, India, I'd love it if you could come up with something. Why don't you brainstorm some ideas? Give me a call if you come up with something.' And then he hung up.

'So much for his input,' I said as I clicked Joe's phone shut.

Joe laughed. 'I take it he, er . . . delegated all the responsibility to you.'

I nodded.

'Mr Non-commitment – that's Baz.' Joe put his hand on my arm. 'Great at passing responsibility down the line. Don't worry. We have loads of time. It's only a couple of painted canvas cloths in the end.'

I put my hand over his. 'Thanks for being so supportive, Joe, I really appreciate it,' I said. Just at that second, Mia appeared around the corner and Joe pulled his hand away, but not before she'd noticed. I saw her stiffen as she approached us, then linked her arm through Joe's and gave me a curt nod.

'Later,' said Joe as he was dragged off with her to join my scenery team.

'Later,' I replied. *I'm not going to run away like a frightened rabbit*, I decided and I sat on the wall opposite the others and got my mobile out to text Erin.

As I was texting in my message (which basically said *Heeeeeeeelp*) I was aware that a couple more people came out of the prefab. Amongst them was Callum Hesketh, and I noticed him glance my way then pull away from the group he was with to come over to me.

He flashed me a kilowatt smile that revealed Hollywood-white teeth. 'New girl,' he said. 'How's it going?'

Part of me wanted to tell the truth and blurt out that I was having a crap day and a crap week and had no friends and felt like a total loser, but I remembered Erin's golden rule for meeting new boys. Be fun, be flirty in the beginning, as boys don't want to hear if you're feeling desperate and it might give them the idea that you're a miserable git all the time.

I flashed Callum a smile back. 'Excellent,' I said.

Callum sat on the wall next to me and I noticed Andrea look over and narrow her eyes. In fact, as I scanned the group opposite I noticed that Andrea wasn't the only one watching. Joe was watching too. And Mia was watching him. I turned my body as if to give Callum my whole attention.

'So what you doing here?' I asked.

Callum jerked a thumb back towards the prefab. 'Rehearsal.'

'You're in *The Boy Friend*?'

He nodded. 'You?'

I shook my head. 'In charge of scenery.'

Callum grimaced. 'Shame.'

I gave him a light pinch on the upper arm. 'Hey. You don't know that. You haven't even seen my artwork.'

Callum looked deep into my eyes. 'No, I meant shame you're not in the play. I play the lead, Tony Brockhurst, and he has some snogging scenes and we could have had fun rehearsing until we got it perfect.'

Wow. He's not shy, I thought as I felt myself go pink. And actually the idea of snogging Callum Hesketh gave me goosebumps. He was really attractive, with a lovely wide mouth with a plump bottom lip. Just asking to be kissed. And he was flirting with me. *I should flirt back*, I decided. *Why not?* Joe was with Mia. There was no point in hanging on in the hope that he might suddenly become free. He had his arm casually draped over her shoulder. He looked comfortable with her. I had to move on.

'I guess we could have,' I said. 'But . . . just because I'm not in the play doesn't mean I couldn't give you some extra-curricular coaching.'

Callum laughed a deep throaty laugh and across the road I could see Joe glaring. *See Joe Donahue*, I thought. *Some boys find me attractive. So there!*

'India Jane,' said Callum, 'I do believe we need to make a date to do just that.' He put his arm around my waist, pulled me to him so that we were really close. He looked at my mouth with hunger and I felt a shiver ripple through me. I thought he was going to kiss me right there and then in front of everyone, but he didn't. He just looked at my mouth for a few moments, as if memorising it, and then he looked into my eyes – and boy, did I feel some chemistry. Like my whole body went into meltdown. A voice in my head started talking gibberish, like *Yabberdabbiedoobie, yeah, mmmm, cor, lovely duckie yumskie yeah . . .* I forced it to shut up and pulled back a little.

'Haven't you got a rehearsal to go to?' I asked.

He sighed and looked over at his audience on the other side of the road. 'I guess, Bailey gave us a five-minute breather,' he said then he got out his phone. 'Give me your number.'

I was about to blurt it out, but then I remembered Erin's second golden rule. If you can get a boy's phone number instead of giving him yours, you will avoid that awful 'Will he? Won't he? When will he phone?' phase as you will be in control of the situation. I got out my phone. 'Tell you what, Mr Hesketh, why don't you give me *yours* instead and I will call you when I feel that the time is right for your tuition.'

Callum raised an eyebrow as if amused by what I had said, then he took my phone and punched in his name and number. As he turned to go into the hall, he gave me an appreciative up-and-down glance that made my pulse quicken. Then he smiled and gave me a brief nod. 'Cool,' was all he said.

Cool is the last word I would use for how I feel. More like hot hot HOT, I thought as I laughed and looked back over the street. Everyone had got up to go apart from Andrea, who was looking at me with pure hate. I didn't care. I flashed her a big smile. I was going to go on a date with Callum Hesketh.

A bit further along, I could see Mia and Joe waiting by the bus stop. Even from a distance, I could tell that they'd been arguing. She was standing with her arms crossed and her expression was sullen. He looked slightly stooped and thoroughly fed up. *Not my fault*, I thought as I turned to go home. Things were looking up. Between Mikey and Callum, I was beginning to feel less like Molly No Mates and more like Sally Some. Maybe life at Holland Park High was going to be OK after all.

Chapter 8

Weekend Blues

'I'm ho-ome,' I called as I let myself through the front door, but no one answered. I went through to the kitchen and found a note on the table from Mum saying that she'd gone to the IMAX cinema with Dylan. I raced up the stairs and knocked on Kate's door. Her room was empty. And so was Aunt Sarah's.

I sat on the top step of the stairs. 'I *need* a pet,' I said to the hallway. 'Someone to say hi to when I come home. Sometimes it's lonely and sooo quiet here!' I could hear the grandfather clock ticking away downstairs. A hum from the kitchen, probably from the American fridge down there. *Silent sounds*, I thought. *There's a contradiction.* But it *was* so quiet that you could hear it. I resolved to ask Mum when she got back about getting a kitten. In the meantime, I had a ton of schoolwork to do as I was still struggling to keep up with the syllabus – but first, I had to talk to Erin. Mum gets a special phone deal where you can phone for next to nothing at the weekend so I knew I could get away with a phonecall instead of texting. Luckily she was there and I filled her in on the morning's events.

'So what exactly is the plot of *The Boy Friend*?' she asked. 'Give me the three-line outline.'

'It's set in a school for young ladies. All the girls have got a boyfriend except the lead character, called Polly, and she feels left out . . .'

'Story of my life,' said Erin.

'What about Scott?'

'Last seen in the arms of Mary McClaughin. I am so over him.'

'No!'

'Yes. Anyway, pray continue with ze plot. I need distracting from my sad plight.'

'That's about it. Left-out actress, Polly, seeks boy. She falls for the errand boy, Tony, who delivers her costume. He's played by Callum, by the way. Errand boy turns out to be millionnaire's son.'

'How very convenient.'

'Indeed. Happy ending, everyone gets a proposal, and they sing and dance.'

'Hurrah. I love a happy ending. You could do it Irish, all green with lots of Irish dancing about.'

'Somehow I can't see Callum in green tights. Don't think

they'll go for it. I'm going to ask Aunt Sarah though. I'm sure she'll have a million ideas.'

'Course. Sorted.'

'Sorted.'

'When will you call Callum?'

'Later today or tomorrow. What do you think?'

'*No way!* Are you *mad*? You'll come across as far too eager if you do that. Treat 'em mean to keep 'em keen, that's the motto. Call him later in the week and, better still, accidentally-on-purpose bump into him at school so he can ask why you haven't called and you can be all casual and like, "Oh was I meant to call you? I forgot how we left it". He will be so impressed, especially as he's the school babe and has girls after him all the while. Show him you're different. More of a challenge. Boys like him always want what they can't have.'

'I salute you O Erin, Queen of the Green Lands for you are wise beyond your years when it comes to boys.'

'I know, I just wish I had boys to practise my fantastic skills on over here. I hope you've got loads of prospective lovers lined up for me for half-term. I can't wait to get over there and explore.'

Erin couldn't talk for long as she had to go and meet a bunch of old mates, and once more, I was left on my own. I went into the kitchen and made some lunch – a Ruspoli special: cheese and tuna toastie. After lunch, I went and sat in the living room and flicked a few TV channels, but nothing appealed. I played a tune on the piano. I wandered through the rest of the house.

Went up and played on my computer, and all the while there was a voice in the back of my head saying, *It's the weekend and you're Molly No Mates. Again.*

I set off for the library to get some books for an assignment and on the way noticed several groups of girls and boys hanging out, drinking coffee, gossiping at a bus stop. I even saw Leela and her mates trying on sunglasses at a pavement stall. They were goofing around, having a laugh, as Leela put three pairs on so that she looked mad. Watching them made me feel lonelier than ever, especially when Leela noticed me standing there watching like a sad stalker. I turned away quickly and walked purposefully off down the road. I wondered whether to call Ruby or Nicole. But would that seem like I was desperate? If they'd wanted me to hang out with them, they'd have invited me, wouldn't they? I didn't want to come across as too clingy or sad. I got my phone out to call Ruby then put it back in my bag. I grabbed it again and wrote a text to Nicole then deleted it. I thought about phoning Mikey but I didn't want to encourage him or give him false hope and I also felt it was unfair to use him just because I had no one else.

Arrghhhhhhhhhhh, I thought. *I am in one of the most crowded cities in the world and yet I've never felt so alone. How pathetic is that?*

Snap out of it, said a strict voice at the back of my head that sounded like my old maths teacher back in Ireland. *Stop being so fricking self obsessed.*

Shut up, said another voice.

You shut up, said yet another.

Oh God, I am losing it, said the first voice.

And then I laughed to myself and thought I must tell Erin about my inner arguments. *Like who needs company when there's a coachload of people living in my head?* I decided to have a badge made saying, *Schizophrenics are never lonely*. I could wear another badge next to it, saying, *Oh yes we are*.

I found the books I needed at the library and did a little homework, then after an hour or so I set off to go home. When I got back, I let myself in, went down to Mum's workroom in the basement and began some sketches for my self-portrait project. I played around with the multi-personality idea and even gave some of my more distinctive voices names – like Paranoid Penny and Sensible Sadie and Wimpy Wanda. As always when I get into drawing or painting, I became so engrossed that the time flew by. Around four o'clock, I heard sounds coming from the kitchen. On further investigation, I found that it was Kate and Tom, the boy she got together with when we were in Greece.

'Hi, Tom,' I said.

He'd draped himself in the window seat and, with his longish dark hair, he looked like a moody rock star. He was watching Kate as she poured two glasses of Aunt Sarah's Chablis. He barely glanced at me. 'Hey.'

'India,' said Kate. 'I thought everyone was out.' She didn't look happy about me being there at all.

Oh I get it, I thought. S*he was hoping to have the house to herself.* I certainly didn't want to be held responsible for ruining her afternoon. 'Nope. I'm here,' I said, but I turned towards the door. 'Er, got to go. Got things to do. Busy busy.'

'Oh by the way,' she said. 'Someone called Ruby called earlier. Is that Ruby Jennings from school?'

I nodded. 'You know her?'

'Everybody knows her.'

'You like her?'

Kate shrugged her shoulders. 'Bit full of herself, but she's OK I guess. I haven't really spent much time with her. Anyhow, Tom, let's go.'

He got up and saluted. 'Yes ma'am. See ya, India Jane.' He followed Kate out like he was an adoring fan. I was about to follow after them, but he didn't even look back to say goodbye and shut the door in my face.

'It's *OK*,' I said. 'I can take a hint!' I'd never felt so invisible in my life. I went to the phone in the hall and called Ruby's number. A lady picked up at the other end and told me that she was out and wouldn't be back until the evening. I didn't have her mobile number and I felt it would be weird to call back her house to get it.

I went back down to the basement to finish my drawing and as I did, I thought about my list of things I wanted in a friend again. It was becoming clearer. I did my drawing in shades of blue and in the style of Picasso in his blue period. It was of me curled up, looking sad and I called it 'Weekend Blues'.

Chapter 9

Moving On

I woke up late on Sunday. It was ten o'clock and I'd slept right through. The aroma of bacon was wafting through the house. *Yum*, I thought as I got dressed and dashed down the stairs.

Mum and Aunt Sarah were in the kitchen, both fully dressed, making brunch with Radio Four on in the background. You'd never guess that they were sisters as they are so unalike. Aunt Sarah is small and dark and Mum is tall and willowy. Even their personalities are total opposites. Aunt Sarah, the do-er, was efficient and precise in her movements. Mum, the dreamer, moved gracefully around the work units, like a dancer.

I pulled up a chair and explained the school show to them as they prepared food. 'So what do you think? I asked when I'd finished.

'Oh. Hmm. Let me get back to you. I'd need a while to think

it over,' said Aunt Sarah as she began cracking eggs into a bowl.

'Cool,' I said. I knew she'd come up with something good, and as far as I was concerned, my scenery theme problems were history. Barry and Andrea would be well impressed when I took in a ton of brilliant ideas over the next few weeks.

After a huge breakfast, I went up to do more homework. Schoolwork always makes me hungry so after a few hours, I crept back down to the kitchen to make a sandwich. It seemed like a feast had appeared whilst I'd been upstairs studying. Salads. Quiches. Chicken. Ham. Lemon tart. Apple pie. 'Is it someone's birthday and I've forgotten?' I asked Mum, who was busy chopping tomatoes for a salad. 'What's with all the nosh?'

Mum grinned. 'Surprise guest.'

'Who?'

'You'll see,' she said.

For a mad moment, I imagined that someone had invited Joe. Maybe Aunt Sarah had. She knew his mum well as they worked together. My heart began to beat fast and I wondered whether to dash back upstairs and apply lip-gloss. However there wasn't time as I heard a commotion in the hall and Mum dashed out to greet whoever it was. Seconds later, I heard a familiar voice. 'And where's my Cinnamon Girl?'

'Dad!' I raced out to the hall to find Dad being embraced by Mum and Dylan. He looked wonderful. Tall, handsome and tanned from being in Europe. He beckoned me over with his right arm and we stood in a rugby-scrum hug while Ethan came in behind us with Dad's cases.

'But I thought you had a week or so to go,' I said after he'd almost squeezed the breath out of me.

'I did, but the gods have smiled on me,' he beamed. 'The man I was replacing made an early recovery and I got offered a position with an orchestra over here. An orchestra who is staying here for the season, I might add and . . . hmmm . . . Is that bacon I smell? Lead the way. I'm starving!'

We trooped after him like a bunch of groupies and watched him tuck into the food with the enthusiasm with which he did everything. We were soon joined by Jessica and the twins, and then Lewis, who had made an effort and rolled out of bed for once. Even Kate put in an appearance, albeit a bleary-eyed one. Once again, the kitchen was like a busy café with people talking over each other, catching up, Dad eager to hear everyone's news and tell his own. *These times with all the family together are my best days*, I thought as I watched everyone jabbering away happily. As the frenzy of noise escalated and Dad went out to say hi to the piano in the front room – cue more noise – I looked around and wondered how I could have ever felt lonely here or that the house was too quiet. However, for me there was still one thing missing.

'Hey Mum,' I said. 'Know what we need to complete the party?'

'Ear plugs,' she replied, but I knew she didn't mind the din.

'Nope. We need a pet.'

'Oh India . . .'

'Please, please, please, *please*.'

'Not my decision. It's up to Sarah.'

I looked over at Aunt Sarah, who had retired to the window seat at the back of the kitchen and was reading the paper. She glanced up when she heard her name.

'Can we have a pet, Aunt Sarah? I'll look after it, I promise.'

'Feel free to say no,' said Mum. 'We've taken over this house enough as it is.'

Aunt Sarah smiled. 'I like it. This house was meant to be full of people. And I love animals. We always had a house full of cats when we were growing up, remember, Fleur? We never had a pet here because I'm away so much and Kate would have forgotten to feed it. So let me think about it, hey? I'll get back to you.'

I wasn't sure if I was being fobbed off as Aunt Sarah is very clever and uses her 'I'll get back to you' line often as a diplomatic way out of things. I've heard her do it a few times with people to do with her business.

Our discussion was cut short by the phone ringing. It turned out to be Ruby. She was desperate for my advice and begged that I go round that afternoon. Although yesterday I would have killed for the same invite, today I wanted to stay home and be with Dad and the family.

'My dad's just got back and I've got schoolwork too so I'd really —' I started.

'Oh. Well if you have more important things to do, fine,' Ruby interrupted. 'No matter. Laters.'

And she hung up! When I tried to call back, the answering

machine was on and I still didn't have her mobile number. I felt awful and spent the rest of the day and a sleepless night agonising about whether I'd blown my one chance at having a friend at school.

She was waiting for me at the gate when I arrived at school the next morning. I began articulating apologies and excuses in my head as she waved and approached me.

She linked her arm through mine to walk into school. 'Oh. My. Go-ooood! Thank *goodness* you're here, India Jane.'

'Me? Listen, Ruby, I'm so sorry about yesterday,' I said. 'You really must give me your mobile as I would have come over yesterday . . .'

'Yesterday? Why?'

'You phoned, remember?'

'Oh that? That was then. Loads has happened since then. My life is over,' she declared. 'And honestly, that Nicole, supposed to be my mate, she *would* pick today of all days to be sick, like when I *really* need her.'

'So what's wrong?'

'Oh don't ask. I can't talk about it. It's way too painful . . .'

'No. I meant with Nicole.'

'Oh her. Flu.' She sighed dramatically. I wondered what I was supposed to do or say, when she turned and looked me directly in the eyes. 'His name is Nick Carson.'

And so the floodgates opened about some student who she'd been on a date with at the weekend but who hadn't called her since.

* * *

Over the next few days, Ruby sought me out every lunchtime to listen to her rollercoaster ride with Nick. By the time Nicole returned to school, it was accepted that I was to be included in their breaktime hang-outs. I didn't push it. In fact, on the first day that Nicole was back, when I saw her with Ruby in their favourite spot near the radiator on the corridor to the art room, I headed off into the canteen.

I spotted Dylan at a corner table. He didn't notice me. He was surrounded by a group of girls and boys and was making them all laugh. I had no worries for him any more. He was already one of the most popular boys in his class. I bought a tuna mayo sandwich and bottle of water, and tried to look as if I was happy to be on my own as I had my lunch, but I still felt conspicuous. Instead of sitting there looking lonely, I decided to go to the library to read over *The Boy Friend* again. The next day was to be the second meeting about the show and although I'd read the script through several times, I was hoping that inspiration would strike. It certainly hadn't so far.

Ruby and Nicole appeared as I was engrossed in the script.

Ruby took a seat next to me and pulled the script out of my hands. 'Hey Lady McSwot,' said Ruby. 'What you doing in here?'

I explained that I'd been put in charge of the scenery and needed to get ideas.

'You've got weeks to think of something,' said Ruby and she tugged on my arm for me to get up and follow her out. 'Come on. Nicole hasn't got your patience *à la* Nick and I *really* need to talk through with you what I'm going to wear tomorrow night.'

Nicole looked slightly hurt for a nano-second, but she covered it quickly and yawned. 'Well, what do you expect? Yada yada. With Ruby, it's always another day, another boy.'

'Nick is different. I think he may be my soul mate,' Ruby objected.

'Yeah. And so was Dan. And Ben. And Michael. And Elliot . . . Need I continue?'

'But I love Nick with a love that is *true*,' said Ruby and she stuck her tongue out at Nicole, who gave me an exasperated look. 'So are you coming?'

'But what about the scenery?'

Ruby picked the script up and put it back on the shelf. 'You said yourself that Bailey said that you have until after half-term. That's years away. Now come on,' she said and they dragged me out to join them at the radiator spot. I didn't mind. In fact, I felt flattered to have been sought out by two of the coolest girls in our year.

'So,' said Ruby. 'Do you think I should go casual student with a touch of bohemia, or more preppy USA?'

'Hmm,' I replied. 'A touch of bohemia? That can be nasty, although I do believe you can get a cream at the chemist's for it.'

Ruby regarded me for a few moments as if she was sizing me up, and under the cold directness of her gaze, I wondered if everyone in the school suffered from a sense of humour failure but then she laughed. 'I get it. Hey. You're funny,' she announced.

Nicole gave a smug look. 'Told you she was,' she said and gave me a conspiratorial wink.

Ruby nodded. 'Case of bohemia. Yeah. Hah. I'll use that.'

'We could try it to get off sports,' said Nicole. 'Hey Miss, I'm coming down with a nasty case of bohemia.'

Ruby didn't laugh. She'd moved on. 'So anyway, India Jane. What do you think? Casual, preppy or slutty?'

And so we spent the rest of the break discussing what look is best for a fourth date. We settled on casual with a touch of slut.

Although Ruby seemed especially keen to spend time with me and made me feel like my listening ear and my advice, in particular, were valuable, Nicole appeared to be more reticent.

'Ruby may seem like she's listening, but she'll do exactly what she wants,' she warned me one afternoon as we made our way out of the school gates. 'You wait and see.' I got the feeling that she was jealous about the way Ruby sought me out now and she was being pushed to the sidelines. I did what I could to ensure that Nicole was included in everything we did though, as the last thing I wanted to do was to cause trouble. My philosophy has always to be totally open about everything to do with mates, so towards the end of the week, I decided to come out and confront it.

'Nicole, I really hope you are OK with me hanging out with you guys,' I said as we walked out of school after classes.

Nicole shrugged. 'Yeah. Whatever.'

'Are you sure? Because I'd hate to cause any friction.'

'Ruby always does exactly what she wants, and she wants you around.'

'I know. But what about you? What do you want? Are you OK with me coming along? I'd really like to be friends with both of you but I know some people would think two's company, three's a crowd.'

Nicole coloured ever so slightly so I knew that I'd hit a nerve. 'Yeah. Maybe,' she said with a flick of her hair, something that I realised she did a lot when she was feeling uncomfortable.

'I just wanted to say that it's your call. If you don't want me around, or if it's making you feel unhappy in any way at all, tell me.'

Nicole looked surprised, but didn't say anything for a few moments.

'OK, think about it then, hey?' I said, and I turned to go off to join Dylan, who was walking on the pavement a short distance ahead with one of his many new mates.

'No, India,' Nicole blurted. 'I'm cool. And . . . thanks for asking.'

I turned back. 'Cool,' I said. 'So, mates?'

Nicole considered me, then nodded and smiled. 'Yeah. Mates,' she said. 'Course we are. And . . . I appreciate that you asked. I mean with Ruby, much as I love her and you know I do, she can be a bit me me me. It's nice someone asked what I want for a change. Like, we both know that Ruby can be demanding and a drama queen, yeah?'

'Yeah. Teen Queen. That's Ruby.'

Nicole nodded. 'Totally. Like some days it's like we live on Planet Ruby and no one else exists, yeah? So you and me should stick together.'

I nodded. That wasn't quite what I'd meant, and I certainly hadn't meant to get into slagging off Ruby, but I didn't want Nicole to think that I was being unnecessarily difficult. *Making new friends can be complicated*, I thought as I headed off.

At home, Aunt Sarah had pulled out a huge pile of art and design books for me to browse through and I found a number of different themes: goth, sci-fi, jungle, fairyland, Aztec, Chinese, beatniks, Renaissance, Victorian . . . I was sure Barry would go for one of them. Over the next week, I took in pages and books to show him, but there was nothing that he saw that he found inspiring.

'I'm not being difficult,' said Barry after I'd given him my latest batch of ideas (including nineteen-fifties' rock and roll), 'but this is my first time at this so we need to do something original, yeah?'

'Er, yeah,' I said. *Easier said than done*, I thought.

Some of the others from the group sent me their ideas and I dutifully passed them on, but there was nothing that grabbed Barry. As half-term loomed closer, I was starting to feel desperate. Joe wasn't any help. I saw him around school, but he didn't pay me much attention and I got a strong feeling that

Mia had told him to stay clear of me. He certainly wasn't his usual friendly self. Andrea seemed to be enjoying my ideas being turned down immensely and gave me a totally fake smile when I saw her in the girls' loos one afternoon. I gave her one back. It wasn't over yet. I'd find Barry his award-winning theme if it was the last thing I did. That would show her and him and the rest of them.

At the weekend, I went through the books that Aunt Sarah had looked out for me again. I also searched the Internet for good themes.

'Call one of your new mates,' Dylan suggested, when I went into the kitchen to make myself a cup of hot chocolate.

I called them both. The answering machine was on at Nicole's, and Ruby's mum picked up and told me that she'd gone out with Nicole. My stomach tightened when I heard that and a chorus of paranoid thoughts burst into my mind like water out of a dam.

Nicole told me that she was going to be at home all day Saturday and wouldn't be seeing Ruby.

Ruby said that she had family stuff on.

Maybe it was a last-minute thing?

I checked my mobile to see if there were any missed calls. Nothing.

Don't be so paranoid, India, we're only just new mates. There must have been loads of weekends when they did stuff together before I came along.

Why should they have invited me?

But maybe I've imagined that we're mates?

Or maybe I've only been half accepted, like a weekday mate. A school mate, but not to be seen out with in public at the weekend?

Oh no! Have I offended one of them? Nicole probably – she hates me.

Or are they just fair-weather friends and only there when it suits them?

Oh God, arrrrgggghhhhhhhhhhhh.

Shut up, mind, shut up all of you.

Chapter 10

Complications

Something weird had happened to my dad.

I looked out of the window on Sunday morning to see him sitting cross-legged with a blanket over his head in the middle of the lawn.

'What is Dad doing?' I asked Mum.

'Meditating,' she said.

'But that's *my* thing,' I said.

'Not any longer,' said Mum with a smirk.

'But why has he got a blanket over his head?'

'Keeps out distractions, or so he says, and helps keep him warm.' She looked out of the window and up at the grey sky. 'Anyhow, India, when did you last practise your meditation?'

'Er . . . few weeks ago,' I lied.

Actually, despite my best intentions, I hadn't meditated since

I was in Greece. When I was over there, I went through an emotional rollercoaster after I'd been shown how to do it by Sensei, the teacher, and after struggling in the early sessions, I had realised that if you stick with it, you feel better. Like an inner battery has been recharged. Trouble was, I *hadn't* stuck with it. Life, school and finding blooming set-painting ideas had taken over.

I helped myself to yogurt and pumpkin seeds and grated pear (my latest favourite breakfast) and as I was eating it, the back door opened and Dad came in beaming and rubbing his hands. 'Marvellous stuff,' he said.

'But it's cold out there,' I said.

'Bracing,' he replied. 'We should do it together.'

No way am I sitting out in the middle of the lawn in October, I thought, *and especially not with a blanket over my head. The neighbours will think we're bonkers.* 'Since when have you been meditating?' I asked.

'Since I came to see you in Greece. I thought we could both do it. A bit of peace of mind never hurt anyone. I've learned all sorts of techniques since. I'm off into the front room now to practise another method.'

Off he went and, moments later, the sound of very loud humming permeated the ground floor. Kate and Aunt Sarah soon appeared.

'What the hell is that din?' asked Aunt Sarah.

'Dad. Meditating,' I replied.

'Can't he do it quietly?' groaned Kate.

'When has Dad ever done anything quietly?' I asked.

Aunt Sarah stormed out. 'He will this. It's Sunday morning. Time for peace and quiet.'

I had to laugh as I straight away heard them arguing. *So much for meditation bringing peace*, I thought as Dad skulked in looking like a little boy who'd had a telling off. Aunt Sarah could be scary when she wanted.

After breakfast, Dad and I took a stroll down to Portobello Market, which was heaving with thousands of tourists and bargain hunters browsing the many and varied stalls there. It was great fun to push and shove with the rest of them and Dad bought me a rose quartz bracelet and he bought a drum (for yet another type of meditation he wanted to try).

'Best experiment when Aunt Sarah's out,' I said.

He nodded and put on a Native American headdress that was lying on a nearby stall. 'Big chief understand,' he said. 'No noise Sunday morning. Big chief Sarah – she no like.'

I laughed. It was good to have him back.

When we got home after the market, Dylan informed me that I had a guest and that Lewis was entertaining her in the living room. I went in to find the most extraordinary sight. Ruby was lying on her back on the floor in front of the fireplace with her arms up behind her head. She had such a teeny top on that it had ridden up to show her perfectly flat stomach and the ruby navel stud she wore. Lewis was sitting squeezed into the corner of the adjacent enormous sofa, looking terrified. I almost burst out laughing when I saw their body language. His arms and legs were crossed like he was trying to protect himself and keep her out. In contrast, she was lying in front of him, open as a book, as if inviting him to leap on top of her.

'Ruby, what are you doing here?' I asked.

Ruby sat up immediately. 'Hey, India. Yeah. We need to talk,' she said and glanced at Lewis.

Lewis was up and out in a flash. 'No prob. Later.'

Ruby shot him a flirtatious look then, when the door shut behind him, she looked back at me. 'Divine boy. Single?'

'Sort of,' I replied. I didn't want to tell her that Lewis always had a girl with him but never seemed to commit to any of them.

'Gorgeous, but all your family are good-looking,' she said as she indicated photos in frames on the piano. 'So romantic. I had a nose about. Hope you don't mind.' And then, as if adjusting her role and remembering the part she wanted to play, she stared at the floor and looked sad.

'So what is it?' I asked.

Ruby sighed. 'Difficult.'

'Try me.'

She looked directly at me. 'OK. I'll just come out with it. So what have you been saying to Nicole?'

'About what?'

'Me.'

'You?'

'Me.'

I scanned my mind. 'I . . . I don't know. I can't remember. Why? What did she say I said?' I asked. I was starting to feel uncomfortable.

Ruby heaved a sigh again and leaned back against the arm of the sofa that Lewis had just vacated. '*She* said that *you* said that *I* was demanding. Always going on about myself, like me me me, and that I acted like a teen queen. *Is* that what you think?'

I was shocked. That sounded more like what Nicole had said. I was about to protest and fill her in that it was her mate who had said that, but I bit my lip just in time. *Be careful*, I thought, *be very careful*.

Ruby was waiting for my reply. I wasn't going to rat on Nicole. I had a feeling that she was trying to stir up trouble. I had come across girls like her before – girls who get you into their confidence, get you to open up, and then use it against you. I made a mental resolution never to open up to Nicole about anything that mattered. In the meantime, I decided that the best course of action was to make light of it. 'Oh that,' I said. 'Oh for heaven's sake, Ruby, you *are* a drama queen. Teen queen supreme. You *know* you are. I haven't said anything to Nicole that I wouldn't say to your face.'

'So you did say it?'

I shrugged. 'I can't remember what I said. Yes, we were talking about you the other day, but neither of us said anything in a negative way. We love you, you know we do. Come on, Ruby. You can't believe that I would be ganging up on you behind your back.'

Ruby pouted. 'That's what Nicole seemed to be insinuating.'

'No way. She must have read it the wrong way. Maybe she's feeling insecure. I mean, it was just the two of you and now I've arrived on the scene. I wouldn't blame her.'

Ruby nodded. 'Yeah. She can be Queen of Paranoia some days.'

'We all can,' I said. 'But honestly, I promise you one thing: I will always say what I think to your face.'

Ruby regarded me for a while. 'That's what I thought. I thought you were on the level. Pff. Nicole. Jesus, it's probably PMT or something.'

'Probably,' I said. 'I turn into psycho woman some months and think that the whole world is plotting against me.'

Minutes later, we were chatting happily again and Ruby seemed to have forgotten what Nicole had said, but I felt that part of me had closed up a fraction. Like an inner wall had gone up. A feeling that was backed up later when Ruby went home and Lewis came out of hiding in Dylan's room.

'Has Spider Woman gone?' he asked.

I nodded. 'Spider Woman? Why? Don't you like her?'

'Stunning,' he said. 'Sexy. But I find predatory girls like that *way* scary. High maintenance. Not my type. Like she's weaving a web to draw you in and then once you're hooked, she'd destroy you.'

I laughed at him. 'You've watched too many sci-fi movies. Anyhow, she's like four years younger than you. How can she be scary?'

'She'd eat me for breakfast and spit out the bones,' he said. 'I like girls who are easier to be around. You watch yourself with her, India.'

I laughed, but I would take on board what he said, to a degree.

A couple of hours later, Nicole phoned. She sounded upset. 'Ruby said she'd been round.'

I felt the queasy feeling in my stomach again. 'Yeah.' *Oh, here we go again*, I thought.

'And she told me what you said.'

'What? I didn't say anything.'

'Not what Ruby said.'

'OK. So what did Ruby say?'

'That you said that I was psycho woman and stirring it because you thought I felt insecure. How could you, India? I took you into my confidence and you've turned it against me.'

'Wha . . .? Na . . .? But Nicole . . .'

'I thought we were friends.'

'We *are*.' I thought she was going to hang up, but she didn't and I went through exactly what I'd said. And what Ruby had said. And what I'd said in reply. Over and over until finally Nicole sounded OK.

'So, mates?' I said.

'Mates,' she said.

Bollards, I thought after we'd hung up. *And I thought I was over-sensitive!* I was going to have to tread carefully with both of them. I decided to go back to the market to buy a present for each of them, to show that there were no hard feelings. I bought a couple of make-up bags for them that were covered with tiny buttons and shells. As I was about to leave, I saw some fab-looking chocolates. *Maybe I'd better buy a stash for emergencies*, I thought as I handed over the last of my pocket money. I had a feeling I was going to need them, with my two new friends.

Chapter 11

Boy Trouble

'*Ah nam myoho renge kyo. Nam myoho renge kyo. NAM MYOHO RENGE KYOOOOOOOO. NAAAAAAAAM . . .*'

'*Dad!* It's six-thirty in the morning! People are trying to sleep,' I called into the living room, where Dad was sitting cross-legged in front of the fireplace.

'Then they're missing the day,' he said and beckoned me into the room. 'Come on, join me. I'm doing a new meditation.'

'Sensei said that while prayer is talking to God, meditation is listening,' I said. 'With that din you're making, he's probably left the universe.'

'Meditation is listening to God? Hmm,' said Dad and, for a moment, I thought I might have made him see sense, but no, a second later, he shook his head. 'So I guess this is singing to God. Probably makes a change for him. *EEEEE NAM*

MYOHO RENGE KYOOOOOOOO.'

Grrrrr, I thought as I went back up to take a shower. The novelty of having Dad back had soon lost its appeal. I had forgotten what a totally *loud* person he can be. He was lucky that Aunt Sarah was away in Greece, closing up her centre for the winter. Like me, she wasn't a morning person. Neither was Kate, by the look of the angry face that appeared on the first floor.

'Can somebody please shoot him?'

'I'll look in the Yellow Pages,' I said, 'and see if I can book someone in. Someone from pest control ought to do it.'

'See if they do early-morning calls. Puhleese.'

'So what's happening with lover boy?' asked Dylan as we strolled into school later that same morning. Joe had just overtaken us on his bike and waved.

'None of your business,' I replied. I was still feeling tired and irritated from the rude awakening from Big Chief Umpalumpa, aka my father.

'Ah. Then you won't be interested in the fact that he's split up with his girlfriend?'

That stopped me in my tracks. 'What do you mean? Joe has? You mean Joe Donahue? How do you know? What do you know?'

Dylan tapped the side of his nose and grinned in an unbelievably annoying way. 'None of my business. Yes. You're quite right. Won't mention it again.'

Sometimes having a younger brother can be *really* frustrating.

'If you don't tell me, I will have to beat you.'

Dylan laughed and pointed at the swarm of pupils heading in through the gates. 'What? Like here on the pavement? In front of half the school?'

'Yeah, I will. You know I will. Just dish the dirt, will you? And how do you know anything about Joe Donahue anyhow?'

'My mate Gareth lives next door to Mia and . . . No, none of my business. La la la la laaaaaah.' He looked positively gleeful about having something that I wanted. I grabbed his neck with both hands and pretended to strangle him.

'Tell me, or you're a dead man.'

A couple of Sixth-Form girls ahead of us saw what I was doing and one of them looked alarmed and rushed over.

'It's OK, he's my little brother,' I said through gritted teeth. 'And he's being a *total* eejit.'

'What's he done?' she asked.

'*Important* boy information that he *won't* tell me,' I said as I continued to strangle.

The girl nodded. 'Hmm. That's bad. I have an annoying brother too. Go right ahead. Batter him for me,' she said over her shoulder as she went to rejoin her friend.

Dylan looked indignant. It was great. 'Oi! You older ones are supposed to *protect* us younger ones,' he called after her.

The girl turned and raised an eyebrow. 'You look like you can look after yourself, squirt.'

Dylan looked as if he was about to explode. 'Squirt? *Squirt!* I hate girls. Life can be so, *so* unjust some days.'

'Tell me about it,' I said as I let him go. 'Now give me the gossip or prepare to die.'

Dylan pouted. 'OK, but under duress. And I get the remote control on the big telly in the living room this weekend.'

Nothing was ever simple with Dylan. 'OK. Fine. Deal.'

'Well . . . my mate Gareth said he overheard Mia talking to her mate on the bus home and she said that her and Joe had finished . . .'

'Who dumped who?'

'Joe. Said he wasn't ready for commitment.'

I punched the air. 'Yesss!'

'Er, dork-brain? Not ready for commitment. That would probably mean you too.'

At that moment, a black Mercedes drew up beside us and Callum Hesketh got out of the passenger seat and waved goodbye to the woman driving. He spotted me and came straight over. 'Ah the lovely India Jane,' he said. 'I've been waiting for your call.'

'Call? Oh. Was I supposed to call you?' I asked as I gave him a mysterious smile. I was pleased that I'd remembered to say exactly what Erin had told me. Cool, cool, cool, that was me.

Dylan elbowed his way in between us. 'Yeah. You were,' he said. 'You told Erin about it remember? On email? And later I heard you again on the hall phone.'

Callum burst out laughing while I felt myself blush. I gave

Dylan a 'get lost' look but he just stood there between us, grinning. I wanted to kill him. Not mock-strangle. Kill. I also wanted the ground to open up and swallow me. 'You shouldn't read other people's emails,' I said, then turned back to Callum. 'I must have been telling my mate about the play and who was in it, you know . . .'

'Yeah. Good. I like to hear that I'm being talked about,' said Callum with a smirk.

'You weren't. At least you were, but only because . . . Oh never mind . . .' My cool act had dissolved like an ice cube in a microwave. Luckily, Callum didn't seem to care. He was staring at my mouth like he wanted to eat it, and it gave me goosebumps all over. Suddenly I didn't care what Dylan had said.

'So, coaching lessons. Remember?' asked Callum with a lopsided grin.

The fact that Dylan was standing between us like a midget chaperone didn't matter one bit. Callum's mouth was like magnet, drawing me towards him. I made myself look away and take a breath.

I got the feeling that he was feeling the same as I was.

'OK, for heaven's *sake*, get a *room*,' said Dylan and he slouched off towards the school gates.

Callum and I both laughed. 'So, when?' he persisted. 'How about we meet here after school and we go and get a cappuccino.'

'Er . . . yeah. OK.'

'Excellent,' said Callum. 'I've got a quick meeting so I'll be like, fifteen minutes after the bell – is that OK?'

'I guess.'

'OK. I'll meet you . . .' He pointed to the church at the corner of the road on the opposite side. 'Outside St Cuthbert's. OK?'

I nodded.

'OK. It's a date,' said Callum and, with a last twinkle, he hooked his rucksack up on to his shoulder and headed inside.

I caught up with Dylan, who was waiting by the gate.

'India Jane Ruspoli,' he said in a prim voice. 'One minute it's all "Oh Joe Donahue, I love him with a love that's true" and *two* seconds later, you're falling over some other guy. Honestly, you're a . . . you're a . . . *slut*.'

My skin was still tingling from the vibe between Callum and me. 'Yeah. That's me. Great isn't it?' *If this is how I feel just looking at Callum*, I thought, *what's it going to be like kissing him? So what if he's got a reputation as a Casanova? I can handle it.*

Dylan gave me a withering look like I was dog poo, but that only made me laugh even more, then he flounced off like a girl. I headed inside too and as I rounded the corner near where people park their bikes, I bumped into Joe.

'Oops, sorry,' I blurted.

'My fault and . . . actually, India, I wanted to . . . that is, about the set design meeting, I . . . er . . .'

'You've been ignoring me. Yeah, I got it.'

Joe smiled. 'I know . . . well, not exactly ignoring you. It's been a weird few weeks and I know . . . I could have been more supportive. Sorry. Been going through some stuff lately . . .'

'Oh, like what? I asked, knowing perfectly well what, thanks to my own personal gossip columnist, Dylan the dirt ditcher.

'Oh nothing, you know, stuff.'

I nodded. Stuff. Boys are such crap at communicating sometimes.

'So any more ideas for Barry?' he asked.

I shook my head. 'I've given him loads, but he just says no, find me something else, something no one has ever done before.'

'He's a cheeky bugger putting it all on you,' said Joe. 'He's the director.'

'That's what I thought.'

Behind us, I noticed Mia and Andrea come through the double doors into the playground. Mia clocked us and swerved to the right, taking Andrea with her. She didn't look pleased to see Joe with me.

Joe hadn't seen her and carried on chatting. 'And I . . . er . . . I noticed you were gassing with Callum before.'

'Yeah.'

'OK. Just, India . . . can I say something about him?'

'Sure.'

'Be careful about him. He has a reputation for messing girls about.'

'You're one to talk.'

'Me? Since when?'

'Oh . . . I heard you were a player, in fact you told me yourself

120

that you were a bad boy before you starting dating Mia.'

'Yeah but . . . different to Callum. I . . .well, you don't need to know what I got up to, but with Callum, I'm telling you for your own good. You seem like a nice girl, genuine, and I don't want to see you getting hurt.'

I felt flattered that Joe would try to warn me, not that I couldn't look after myself. I got that Callum wasn't a boy to give your heart to. Not if you wanted it to stay in one piece. That wasn't to say I couldn't snog him. No point in totally missing out. But Joe warning me off? Did it mean that he was interested me?

'Oh really. You do realise that this is the second time you've told me to steer clear of a boy.'

'Who else?'

'Liam.'

'Oh yeah, that guy in Greece. Well, he was a creep.'

After my encounter with Callum, I was feeling more confident than usual and I moved slightly closer to Joe. 'You wouldn't have an ulterior motive for keeping these other boys away?' I said in a low soft voice.

Joe looked right into my eyes and I could tell he didn't mind me moving closer. His eyes filled with mischief. 'Why? Just what are you suggesting, Miss Ruspoli?' he asked.

For the second time that morning, I got goosebumps. 'I . . .' My reply was drowned out by the bell for assembly that rang about a metre away from us, causing us to almost jump out of our skins. The playground began to fill pupils with heading inside.

121

Joe shrugged, smiled, and took a step back. 'Later,' he said. And at last, I felt we were back where we left off at the end of the holidays. He'd said the same word at the airport after we'd spent the flight gabbing away. *Later.* But it was a loaded later.

Yabbadabbadoobie. What a start to the day, I thought as I caught sight of Ruby and Nicole coming towards me.

'Boys are like buses,' I said when I joined them. 'You wait for ages for one and then two come along at the same time.'

'Yeah,' said Ruby and without asking what I meant, launched into her latest episode of what was happening on Planet Ruby.

I didn't mind. I had two of the most gorgeous boys in the school interested in me and I spent the whole day floating between fantasies about them. *Callum or Joe? Well, I am a Gemini*, I told myself. *The sign of the twins, so they can have one each!* My inner glow of happiness lasted exactly until the last period of the day, which was art. I arrived a few minutes early and Mia was the only other person there.

'Hi,' I said, giving her a bright smile.

She didn't reply. *That is so not fair*, I thought as I found myself a drawing board and paper. *I don't deserve this. I didn't ask Joe to dump her or even encourage him in any way at all before he did.*

'Mia, what's the matter?' I asked as I took a place next to her.

'I think you know,' she said without looking at me.

'Actually, I don't.'

Mia turned her back to me.

'Listen, Mia, we have to be together in art until the end of the year. I really think we ought to try and get on.'

'We don't have to,' she replied.

'But I don't get it, Mia. I haven't done anything and if this about Joe, I haven't done anything to come between you.'

'Then how come we were getting along fine until you arrived,' she said, suddenly turning on me.

'I've no idea, but I really don't think you breaking up had anything to do with me. Honestly.'

'So you know then? I suppose it's all round the school that he dumped me.'

'Noooo. I doubt it. I really do, and I'm sorry you broke up.'

'Yeah, right,' said Mia and as others began to arrive for class, she got up and shifted her stuff again so that she was sitting as far away from me as possible.

For the rest of the class, I did a self-portrait which resembled a painting that Lewis used to have on his bedroom wall when he lived with us in Ireland. It's called 'The Scream' by a painter called Edvard Munch and is of an agonised figure in black, with a skull for a head depicted against a blood-red sky. The skull has a toothless mouth open, screaming. I painted myself in place of the figure, wide mouth open in a silent scream.

'Hmm. Interesting,' said Mr Bailey when he came round to look at everyone's work. 'Bad day, huh?'

'What do you think?' I asked.

Mr Bailey laughed. 'Oh the angst of you teenagers,' he said like it was all one big joke. 'How's the set-painting coming along?'

'Like a slow train on the track to nowheresville.'

Mr Bailey cracked up again like I was the funniest comedian he'd ever met. 'Excellent, excellent,' he said. 'Carry on.'

After school, seeing as I had fifteen minutes before meeting Callum, I called Nicole's mobile to see if maybe she and Ruby were still around. I wanted to see them both and tell them about Mia and Joe. Hear what they thought. Hopefully get a bit of matey-type support.

'Oh hi,' said Nicole flatly when she picked up.

'Hi. Just wondered where you guys were.'

'Busy busy, you know. We've got to get the latest edition of the school magazine out and it's giving us total nightmares.'

I was about to say that I'd come and help, when Nicole said, 'Got to go. Toodles.' And she hung up.

Oh for puke's sake, I thought. *Why didn't they ask me to go with them?* asked my inner Paranoid Penny. *I bet that they've been talking about me again and no doubt taken something I've said the wrong way.*

Oh shut up, said Sensible Sadie. *Stop obsessing.*

All I want is to have friends that liiiiiiike me, said Wimpy Wanda.

I ran my fingers through my hair. *Oh God, the voices are back*, I thought. *I need to meditate. That's what I need*. I remembered what the teacher in Greece had said about the mind being like the sea and on the surface were waves, sometimes choppy, sometimes calm, but whatever was happening on the surface, deep deep down was peace. I needed to feel that, so I decided to go into the church where I was supposed to be meeting

Callum and attempt to meditate my way back to sanity.

I made my way down the road and up to the church doors. Luckily they were open. I was immediately struck by the smell of frankincense. I recognised the scent because Mum used it in the face creams that she made for Aunt Sarah's shops. Inside, it felt cool and quiet and a welcome contrast to the busy street outside – like someone had pressed the mute button on a remote control. There were a couple of people in there besides me: an old lady at the front who appeared to be doing a rosary and another lady about halfway down. I slipped into a pew at the back and closed my eyes. As I sat there, I remembered Sensei's saying that I'd quoted to Dad, about how prayer is talking to God, meditation is listening.

I made myself focus on my breath in the way that I had been taught. Sensei had given two methods and sometimes I did one, sometimes the other. The first was to be aware of each breath as it went into the body and each breath as it left. Cool air going in the nostrils, warm air going out seconds later. Sensei'd said to breathe naturally, but to watch each breath with the kind of attention that a sentry on a gate would watch people going in and out – aware of each one. The second method was to shift the concentration to the abdomen area. Again we were told to focus on the breath and how, as we breathe in, the abdomen rises slightly, as we breathe out, it falls. For the second method, we were told simply to stay with the gentle rising and falling of the abdomen. It was some ancient Buddhist method apparently. I tried to focus and not to take any notice of the thoughts that drifted in and out. As I sat there, I was aware that my mind was rambling all over the place, thinking about school, Nicole, Joe, Ruby, Kate, the scenery. I checked my watch. Another eight minutes to go before I met Callum. I made myself refocus.

I am still, not my thoughts.

Warm breath in the nostrils, cold breath out. No. No. Idiot, it's the other way around. Breathe cold air in, warm breath out.

Focus, focus.

I wonder if Callum will try and kiss me tonight. And if he does, what should I do? Snog him back or be cool?

Focus. Focus.

But I ought to have some kind of game plan.

That's true. Should I kiss him back or would that make me seem easy?

Hmm.

I wonder if anything will ever happen with Joe and I?

FOCUS, INDIA. YOU ARE SUCH CRAP AT STICKING WITH THIS.

Shut up. Go away, Bossy Knickers.

But you're away with the first thought that flies across your mind. Your concentration is PATHETIC.

Yeah, but can I help it if they come disguised as cute-looking boys?

Oh hell, too many voices. I am mad.

No. It's OK. I'm not. Everybody has this going on in their head. They're only thoughts. I am completely sane, just I have to go beyond, go deeper.

I refocused and then realised that it might be time to meet Callum.

No harm in being late, said a voice that sounded distinctly like Erin's. Join the gang, I said to my inner Erin. *There's a whole pile of them in the back of my head, having a cocktail party.*

I got up to go. As I headed towards the door, I noticed to my left that there was there was a statue of Mary, Jesus's mother, and beside it were notes in different handwriting. My curiosity got the better of me and I had to go and take a peek. As I studied them, I saw that they were prayers.

Please see my father through this sad time since my mother died. He is so lonely now without his lifetime companion. They were together for fifty years and he is lost without her.

For my son Michael who has leukaemia. Dear God, he's only twelve and I hate to see him suffer. Please give him strength to get through this difficult time. And his brother Jamie who doesn't know what to do to make it better and also suffers.

Please God, spare my brother Arthur who is in hospital.

Dear God, forgive me for my recent actions. I have let my family down time and again and feel I am of no worth. I have no job and feel that they despise me. Please help as I have no one else.

One after the other, pleas from the sad, the sick, the lonely, the lost. I felt my eyes fill up with tears. Such simple requests. Straight from the heart.

I noticed that there were sheaves of paper and a pencil beneath the statue. I was about to write a message, but didn't know what to say. *What would I pray for? After reading the messages, I realise that my life is good*, I thought as I glanced at my watch and realised that I was going to be five minutes late and Callum would probably be outside.

I made my way out to the street again, but there was no sign of him. The pavements were quiet, just a few stray pupils making their way out of the gates. I noticed Leela on the other side of the road with her mates, Brook and Zahrah. She looked over and waved, then said something to the others. I waved back and I saw Leela hesitate, as if thinking about coming over, but then Brook linked her arm through hers and they walked on. I wondered what she had been going to come over for. I wished she had. I'd have liked to have had a chance to get to know her better. Ten minutes later, Mikey went past hand in hand with his new girlfriend. He also waved, and behind the girl's back, gave me the thumbs up. *Must be his crush from the French group*, I thought. A part of me felt a twinge of jealousy. Mikey was mine. Like my pet. OK, I didn't want him as a boyfriend, but he made me feel so special, like I was the most attractive and entertaining girl in the world. But then I was never going to go out with him, so I couldn't expect him to wait for me for ever, hanging on my every word and writing poetry about unrequited love. I waved back and hoped that the fact he had a girlfriend now wouldn't mean that we couldn't still be mates.

I waited half an hour. Forty minutes . . . but there was no sign of Callum. I got out my phone to see if there was a message, then remembered that I hadn't given him my number. I quickly dialled his. It was on voicemail.

I felt my heart sink. Stood up on my very first date in London. How pathetic is that?

I tried to call Erin. I got her voicemail. I thought about calling Nicole or Ruby again but didn't fancy another brush off. *I so wish I had someone I could call without any agenda or paranoia about how they're going to react,* I thought as I went back into the church, picked up a pencil under the statue and wrote, *Dear God, if you get these messages, please answer everyone's prayers and please look after my family and Erin and please can I make some good friends at my new school, even just one would do – someone like Erin if that's at all possible. Thanks a lot.*

I Blu-tacked my prayer up with the others and left the church. *I've tried the listening to God bit,* I thought, *now let's see if he's listening to me.*

Chapter 12

Make-do Mates

'What's up, India?' Mum asked when I trooped in the back door later that evening.

'I have been at my new school for almost half a term, everyone hates me, I have no friends, no boyfriend, I have a spot on my chin and no theme for the school play, everyone's depending on me *and* there's a whole pile of people with really sad lives down at the church and I don't understand why there's so much pain in the world and why are we here anyway and why do people have to suffer and die and be lonely. And also, why are there wars and people killing each other? *That* doesn't help and ought to be banned *immediately*.' I'd been thinking *a lot* on the way home.

'Wow, I'll have to think about some of those questions,' said Mum as we heard the phone ring in the hall.

A few seconds later, Dylan brought through the portable handset for me. It was Ruby. She hardly drew breath as she launched into her latest tale of woe (Nick was going rowing at half-term and hadn't asked her to go and watch him). I listened as I drank a cup of hot chocolate, ate the tuna toastie that Mum had made me, cleared the table, arm wrestled with Dylan (he won) – all the while with the phone tucked into the crook of my neck. I tried to interject when I could with words of sympathy like: Who needs him? He doesn't deserve you. Rowing is boring . . . But I could tell that she wasn't really listening. Finally, she heaved a huge sigh. 'Thanks soooo much, India, I feel so much better now.' And she hung up. *She might feel better*, I thought, *but I now have a stiff neck and a headache coming on.*

Mum was watching me thoughtfully as Dylan took the phone and went out into the hall to have a 'private conversation'.

'What?' I asked.

'Was that the girl who was here the other day?'

I nodded. 'Ruby. She's a friend, kind of.'

'Does she always do that?'

'Do what?'

'Talk at you.'

'Suppose.'

Mum looked thoughtful again. 'Does she listen to you when you need to talk?'

I burst out laughing. 'Yeah, right.'

'I thought so. She's very probably a very lovely girl, so don't take this the wrong way, but . . . don't let her take over. It's so easy to let these larger-than-life characters monopolise everything. I should know, I'm married to one. But at least with your dad, he does ask about me, gives me time to talk – but in the early days of our relationship, I lived in his shadow and was happy for him to take centre stage. It's only now that I'm finding my voice. I don't want to see someone overshadow you, that's all I'm saying. You're our Cinnamon Girl and you deserve to shine too.'

I smiled at Mum and gave her a hug. She meant well, but she *so* didn't understand what it was like in school these days. It was either accept my role with Nicole and Ruby or have no one to hang out with. And I did have a true friend, Erin, even if she was at the other end of the phone or via computer, and it wouldn't be long before I saw her as half-term was just around the corner. However, what Mum had said had disturbed me. I didn't want to become invisible, nobody more than a listening ear, with no voice of my own, quietly living in other people's shadows. I needed to reassure myself that wasn't happening so I went up to my bedroom and quickly texted Erin to go to MSN if she was at home. Luckily she was.

Cinnamongirl: O dear absent friend, I must needs speaketh with thou on several matters. For one, I go forth in lamentation, for my love has been forsaken and I shall not make a mating this very day.

Her message came straight back.

Irishbrat4eva: How oddly thou dost thou write? It doth sound that thou are wedded to calamity.

Cinnamongirl: Indeedeth. And I fear I am not likeable at all for I have no proper friends, not maiden nor male.

Irishbrat4eva: Ah this is because thou has known the very best, verily an A-star friend such as me is surely hard to follow. All else are like pale weeds next to a scented rose.

Cinnamongirl: Thou dost speak the truth, indeedie thou dost.

Irishbrat4eva: Fret not and verily and forsooth an all, do not forget that thou art also an A-star friend. Summer has not such a flower as thee.

Cinnamongirl: Thy words are like honey to my ears.

Irishbrat4eva: What? Sticky?

Cinnamongirl: No, idiot. Sweet. But other things dost trouble my mind and I must speaketh of them hence.

Irishbrat4eva: Speak away and awoe too.

Cinnamongirl: This world is a world of pain and shadow and the hearts of many men are broken. For what reason I ask do men draw sword upon the other and add to this pain? And for what reason came we hence?

Irishbrat4eva: We camest to this fair land to experience the rich tapestry of life with all its colours and looms. And as for the woe and the winter, forget not the days of spring and cherry blossom, for each has its opposite and that and all.

Cinnamongirl: Thou speakest true, O fair maiden of the green land. Indeed. For after snow comes the sun. Thou hast remindest me that sometimes one must give the birds of doom that fly over one's head the finger.

Irishbrat4eva: Verily. The one finger. Anyway, I must away.

Cinnamongirl: Me too. The night's clock doth sound that it is time for slumber, so goodnight goodnight till it be morrow.

Irishbrat4eva: Goodnight, goodnight, for soon I will be there and we can rejoice and make merry.

Cinnamongirl: Till then. I must away. Away. Away . . .

I went to sleep that night feeling a whole lot better. So my school friends weren't as good friends as Erin was, but at least I had her, and after reading the messages in the church, I realised that was more than some people in the world.

There were four messages on my phone the next morning. All from Callum.

Sree. Sree. Sree. Cl me.

Keep ur fne on.

India, sree I mssd u. Can xplain.

Meet @ break-time? Outside library.

Of course, I thought as I read the messages. *He must have got my*

134

number from my missed call when I phoned him last night. I debated whether to go and meet him and quickly texted Erin to ask what she thought. Luckily I got her before she'd turned her phone off for school.

Absolutely, she texted back. Good morrow. Nothing ventured, nothing gained. The season for being cooleth is done. Goeth forth, get yon fair knight in shining armani and polish his helmet. OK, maybe not that bit. And a hey nonnie wotsit.

Oh Lord, here we go again, I thought as I went through the school gates. *Another day.*

I was a few minutes early for assembly so I glanced over the school notices before going into the hall. One at the bottom caught my eye.

Homes wanted for kittens. Six weeks old: three boys, two girls. Very cute. Call 084567811.

Excellent, I thought as I noted the number. I could ask Aunt Sarah again. Or even better, just go and get them. She wouldn't be able to resist.

It was double French first thing and it seemed to last for eternity, but at last, the bell went for break and I shot out to the cloakroom to apply some lip-gloss, then made my way to the library. Callum was already there and his face lit up when he saw me.

'The lovely India Jane. More radiant than ever,' he said.

'Cut the crap, Hesketh,' I said.

'Such honeyed words from my love,' he said with a laugh.

I smiled back at him. 'Ah, you speak Shakespearian? Me and

my mate Erin are fluent in yon language.'

'Verily I do, I played Hamlet last year,' he said and he went into a classic Shakespearian pose. 'To be or not to be, that is the wotnot; to sleep, perchance to dream of better things to come, aye give us a rub or something like that. I forget.'

'Bet you looked lovely in tights,' I said.

'I could show you if you want to come home with me one evening.'

I laughed and held up my hand in the stop sign. 'Eww. Visual overload. Sorry. Stick to jeans. So . . . you called to grovel, I presume.'

Callum grinned his lovely lopsided grin. 'I did. I am so *so* sorry I missed you yesterday. Emergency at home. There was no one to let my younger sister in and Mum called and said I had to get back home. I did go to the church early in the hope that you might be early too, but no sign of you, and of course I didn't have your number. So, sorry, sorry – can you forgive me?'

I could tell he was on the level. 'I guess, though it is very tempting to make you do penance.' *It's so weird with Callum*, I thought as I listened to myself flirting outrageously. *With Joe in the summer, until I got to know him better, I became the village idiot every time I spoke to him, but with Callum, I can be myself. I guess it's because I know that it's not going to last.*

'Oh yes, punish me please,' he said in an equally flirtatious way and then he leaned over and kissed me. Right on the mouth. Right in front of everyone. And not a peck or a two-second kiss, a proper snog. With tongues.

'Wuh . . . er . . .' I blustered after a few moments.

'So. My first bit of coaching. Come on. You can be honest. How was it?'

I put on a prim expression. 'Hmm. Yes. You have potential, Mr Hesketh, but . . . I think you need to practise *a lot* more. I prescribe regular sessions.'

Snogging was one of the few things in life that I was reasonably confident about, thanks to Erin. I used to be totally paranoid about it and agonised about whether I'd be any good at it. I mean, everyone has to do it sooner or later, unless you're a nun, but where are you supposed to find out how to be *good* at it? (Come to think of it, nuns probably do get snogged up once or twice before they take their Holy Vows. I like to think so. I don't like to think of them missing out for ever. Although the fact they take a vow of celibacy may be down to the fact that they were kissed once by some slimy whelk-type kisser and thought all kisses were alike – hence a Holy Vow never to kiss again and promise themselves to the Lord Jesus instead.) One day I'd confessed my snog anxieties to Erin. It was about half an hour before we were due to open the doors for a school Christmas fair and we were manning a stall in a small room off the main hall. Quick as a flash, Erin made a sign saying, *Kiss for a Pound*. I kissed seventeen boys that day. Erin stood at the door to make sure no teachers came by. It was a fantastic experience because it showed me that there are *all* sorts of kissers and *all* sorts of kisses. Long, short, hard, light, wet and slimy (ew), dry, passionate, weak and wimpy, shy, confident . . . Erin, who had been kissed before by three boys – although not all at the same time of course – gave me a few tips before we got started. 'Vary the pressure,' she said, 'and relax. Sometimes you take your lead from him. Sometimes you have to lead him, in which case try nibbling his lower lip.' She made me practise for a few minutes on the back of my hand (I felt such a prat but it had to be done) and then we were away. By the end of the day, I was an expert, plus Sister Christina was full of praises for the money that we raised, although she would have died if she'd known that we'd held a snogathon to get it. Erin said that we'd have raised even more if one of the nuns had been willing to give a kiss for a pound, but I had my doubts about that. Sister Christina had a moustache and, if I'm being totally honest, a bit of a beard.

'Practise more? Good,' said Callum, and he moved in for another snog. I took a quick look to see if anyone had noticed us and indeed they had. A few people were watching and as I closed my eyes as Callum's lips touched mine again, it felt brilliant not only to be kissing one of the hottest boys in the school but also to be doing it in full view of —

'INDIA Jane Ruspoli, CALLUM Hesketh!' boomed a familiar voice. 'What on EARTH do you think you're doing?'

We both sprang back to see Mrs Goldman standing in front of us. She looked very upset.

'Er, rehearsing for the school play?' Callum suggested.

'And since when has chewing a fellow pupil's face been a part of a school play at this establishment? Both of you – go to your next lesson and DON'T let this ever happen again.'

We both headed off in opposite directions, but I couldn't resist turning round after a short distance. Callum had turned around too and grinned at me. 'I'll call you,' he mouthed.

Yesssss, I thought as I headed off towards double maths. *Joe Donahue, who needs you?*

Later in the week, we had a second 'coaching' session at lunch break, this time in a more private place – behind the sports equipment in the gym. And a third session after school, behind a tree on the green on the way home.

Snogging Callum was fun. And enjoyable. But I knew that he wasn't The One after the second snog. He was a good kisser, an eight out of ten, but for me, something wasn't right. I could see that he already had a true love. Himself. Ruby had been dead right in her assessment of him. It was him and him and there was no room for anyone else. I could never fall in love with someone like Callum, who was so in love with himself. Plus the fact I got the feeling that he kissed by numbers, like he'd read a 'how to be a great kisser' article in a magazine. He always started by looking at my bottom lip hungrily like he had the first two times we'd met, but the goosebumpy effect it had on me in the beginning soon wore off. I realised that it was step one in his snogging technique and, although good and it worked at first, it wasn't something that should be repeated *every* time. I believed that if what was between us was genuine and passionate, then snogging him would be slightly different every time. However, it was good practise, as Erin would say, and being seen with him was definitely giving me tons of cred about school.

After our third session, he took my hand and looked deeply into my eyes. 'India, I need to talk to you about something.'

'Uhuh,' I said. *Riveting come back. Not. He's going to dump you*, said my inner Paranoid Penny.

'You know I think you're fab . . .'

'Uhuh,' I repeated as my inner Sensible Sadie thought, *You really must work on your conversation skills.*

'Well, I just wanted to make a few things clear and I hope you won't take it personally.'

'OK . . .' I said as my heart beat a little faster and my inner Paraniod Penny perked up even more. *Oh God, here we go,* she groaned. *Dumped by someone you're not even that bothered about!*

'It's just . . . well, last year I was in a serious relationship and I don't want to get involved again so early on and I know that usually, at this stage of the game, girls start thinking that we're an item and expecting . . . you know, dates, little presents, phonecalls . . .'

I burst out laughing. He really was *so* full of himself. 'You think I want a relationship with *you*? *As if.* Look, Hesketh, I've only just got to this school and I don't want to be tied down either so, a relationship with me? Dream on.'

Callum looked totally taken aback and I got the feeling that no one had ever said anything like that to him before. A new-found respect crept into his eyes and he pulled me close again. 'Cool, Ruspoli. Good. So we're on the same page. Now? Where were we?'

Step one, I thought. *You look at my bottom lip.*

And so my new life drifted along. I knew my way around the school. I was almost up to date with my GCSE work and it no longer felt like I was studying totally different syllabuses to my last school. I had my make-do mates, Ruby and Nicole. We got on as long as I had no expectations and made no demands. I got their rules: I went along with *their* plans. I met where it was convenient for *them*. At times that were good for *them*. In between times, I had Mikey to sometimes walk home and have a laugh with and I had my casual boyfriend, Callum, who became keener and keener the more I kept him at arm's length. It wasn't an act either. I wasn't playing at being cool like I tried to do with Joe. I could cope. I could get by. I could compromise if I needed to. I was beginning to fit in.

And then Erin arrived.

Chapter 13

Half-term

Flight BA459 from Dublin had landed over forty minutes earlier. A whole crowd of people had come through Arrivals, but no sign of Erin.

'She's probably been held up at the baggage collection point,' said Dad. 'It can take ages to come sometimes.'

I craned my neck to see as the doors opened and more passengers came through pushing trolleys, scanning the waiting crowd.

Strolling along amongst the latest group of travellers, I noticed a pretty tall blonde girl dressed in jeans, navy Converse All Stars, a three-quarter-length black coat and an enormous blue scarf wrapped around her neck a couple of times. She was with a very attractive boy and was chatting away animatedly. She had an open face and looked like the type of person who you could have a good laugh with. It was Erin.

I felt a wave of pure happiness flood through me and began to wave like mad as Erin's gaze searched the arrival lounge for us. She looked fabulous. Even better than when I left her at the beginning of the summer. Her hair was longer and the terracotta-coloured lippie she was wearing made her look more sophisticated.

'Eriiiiiiiiiiiiiiiiiiiiiiiiiiiiiiin!' I yelled.

She spotted me immediately, her face lit up, and she charged towards us, almost knocking over an old lady in front of her with her luggage trolley. We gave each other a dancing hug.

'You look great,' she said.

'So do you,' I said. 'Totally.'

'Hi, Mr Ruspoli,' she said, flashing Dad a grin. 'Looking good too.'

'Hi, Erin,' said Dad.

'And who's this?' I asked as the boy she'd been chatting to caught up with us.

'Oh, Jamie, this is my mate India who I was telling you about.'

The boy smiled and shoved a note into her hand. 'My numbers. Call me,' he said, then set off towards a middle-aged woman who was waving at him further down the line.

Erin looked at me, raised an eyebrow. 'Nice work, huh?'

'*Fast* work,' I replied.

'We sat on the plane together. I pretended I was soooo nervous so he held my hand. Hahaha. Boys just love to act the big man, yeah?'

Dad rolled his eyes and laughed, took Erin's trolley and wheeled it off towards the short-stay car park.

And then we were off. Nattering, laughing, catching up, not drawing breath as we followed Dad out to Aunt Sarah's BMW. On the way home, we sat in the back and continued our catch up. It was like I had seen her only the day before and, for a brief moment when we were both quiet, I looked out of the window at the traffic on the M4 and thought, *I haven't felt this happy for ages.*

When we got home and she'd done the tour of the house and been through my wardrobe and tried on anything new since I was in Ireland plus all my bracelets, earrings and bits of jewellery, she filled me in on everything about her life lately and I told her everything about my new life in London – about how quiet the house felt sometimes when everyone went about their busy lives, how lonely I felt some days without a real friend, how hard it had been catching up with my schoolwork, how I was supposed to be coming up with an awesome theme for the play and so far hadn't delivered anything, and finally how I'd seen some kittens who needed homes. Erin listened carefully to all of it and once again I realised how much I'd missed her and her genuine interest in me and my life.

'So let's go and meet this Nicole and Ruby,' she said. 'I want to see who you've chosen to replace me.'

'Never *replace*. Ruby's gone to France. And Nicole's visiting her dad down in Bristol. Her folks are divorced.'

'So good job I'm here,' said Erin. 'You'd have been all on your own otherwise.'

I nodded. I didn't tell her that chances were I'd have been on my own even if Nicole and Ruby had been in town.

'You got the number for the kittens?' she asked as she knelt on my bed and looked out of the window at the street down below.

I nodded and pointed at the details I had copied from the school noticeboard and then pinned up on the one I had behind my desk.

'Cool. OK. Let's have some more carrot cake and then go and explore Londonium.'

'Your wish is my command,' I said and disappeared downstairs to refill the tray with goodies we'd got in for her visit.

When I came back with a tray stacked with cheese scones, cake and hot chocolate, Erin was wearing one of my necklaces and a smug expression.

'What?' I asked. I knew that look from old.

'I got us an appointment.'

I felt the old familiar feeling. What was she getting us into now? Over in Ireland, she was always coming up with mad pranks or things to do. She's a Taurus, but has Aries rising, which explains why she rushes into everything headfirst. An appointment with Erin could mean anything from having a tattoo done to doing a dare (usually involving a boy) to pretending to be TV researchers (a great excuse to approach boys).

'Okaaaaay,' I said. 'With who?'

'Kittens,' she said. 'I called the number.'

'But Aunt Sarah hasn't agreed yet.'

'The lady who answered sounded nice.'

'Young or old?'

'Dunno. Old. She asked where I'd got the number and I said from your school and she said come right over. There are three left now so I reckoned we'd better get over there before they're all taken.'

'But Mum will kill me and . . .'

'We're only going to look, India Jane, and if you like one, you can reserve it and then we can both work on your Aunt Sarah when she gets back from land of the feta cheese. Oh come on. If we don't, someone else might get there first.'

I could see her reasoning. 'OK. But we're not going to commit.'

'Course not,' she said.

I looked up the address that she'd been given in my *A–Z* and ten minutes later, we had our jackets on and were on our way. It wasn't far and as we made our way along the streets, Erin fired more questions at me about Callum and Joe and Ruby and Nicole. It felt strange at first – as I hadn't talked so much about myself in ages – but I made sure that I asked her lots of questions back. I really wanted it to be a give-and-take equal relationship. Spending time with Nicole and Ruby had taught me that in a true friendship that it was important to have a balance.

Number fifteen was a semi-detached house on a road not far from Portobello Market. At the front was an open gate and concrete forecourt in which were parked two cars, a silver Fiat and a black Mercedes.

We went up to the door and rang the bell. An elderly Indian lady in a white sari opened the door.

Erin flashed her a big smile. 'We're here to see the kittens,' she said.

The lady smiled back at her and beckoned us inside. 'Come. Come. You're Erin? Yes?' she asked as Erin nodded. 'I'll fetch my daughter. Come. Come.' She held the door for us and we stepped into an immaculate cream hallway with a large Indian figure in the corner. From the four arms, I knew that it was the goddess Kali.

'Pina,' called the old lady and, a few seconds later, an attractive lady with long dark wavy hair appeared. She was dressed in a navy suit and court shoes.

'Hi,' she said. 'Auntie said someone had called. You must be Erin and your friend . . .?'

I laughed to myself. Erin'd only been in London for two seconds and already introduced herself to the neighbourhood on the phone. 'India Jane.'

'Come this way and you can see them,' said Pina. 'We hate to give them away but we have two cats already and can't keep them all.'

She led us into a light airy room at the back of the house and indicated that the kittens were in a box to the left of a brown leather sofa.

Erin was straight over. Like me, she's always loved animals –

at her house back in Ireland, her family have three cats, Beavis, Butthead and Buffy, an old dog called Nellie, a hamster called Spartacus and three black sheep – Beryl, Gloria and Doris.

I followed her over and knelt over the box. 'Ohmigod,' I said as three adorable little faces looked up at us.

'The black-and-white one is a boy and the two tabbies are girls,' said Pina.

I wanted all of them. The black-and-white one was lying on his back and the two girls were curled up together with their paws wrapped around each other.

The elderly lady came in. 'Would our guests like a drink?' she asked.

Erin nodded, so I did too.

'I'll bring you some lemonade,' said Auntie.

Pina handed me a piece of paper that had been tied to a string. 'Here, they love to play with this. I'll go and help Auntie and you get to know the kittens. We haven't named them yet.'

As soon as she'd gone from the room, Erin was up looking at some photos on the mantelpiece. 'These must be her children,' she said. 'Nice-looking bunch. Ooh. And the boy's a cutie.'

'Erin, those are private,' I said, but I couldn't resist going to have a look as well. I went over to join her by the fireplace. 'Ohmigod!'

'What?'

'I know them. I mean her. I mean both of them. The girls.' In the photo were Leela and Anisha, standing with Pina and a handsome-looking boy who looked about seventeen. They looked as though they were at an Indian wedding and were dressed in traditional style. 'Leela goes to my school and I met Anisha in Greece. She works for my aunt over there.'

'Bollywood babes,' said Erin. 'And the brother's a total god.'

'Yeah,' I agreed as we heard the front door open.

'We have guests,' Pina called from somewhere.

'Where?' asked a female voice I recognised as Leela's.

'Come to see the cats. In the back room.'

Seconds later, Leela appeared with Zahrah and Brook. They were dressed in jeans, T-shirts and Converse All Stars (Leela's were pink, Zahrah's green with a stripe, and Brook's were turquoise). They all looked surprised to see me there and I felt totally embarrassed, like I'd been caught going through their private things. Not Erin though.

'Hi,' she said and pointed at the navy Converses she was wearing, then at my red ones. 'Snap. Cool sneakers.'

Leela smiled. 'We're all members of the Converse club, hey? We ought to make up a secret hand sign.'

Erin nodded, made her eyes go crossed then did a strange trembly salute with her right hand. Leela immediately copied her and they both burst out laughing.

'We're here to look at the kittens,' Erin continued. 'They're so totally adorable, already we want all of them. Do you go to India's school?'

And that was it. Like they'd all known each other for ever. Soon they were sitting together on the couch telling jokes, swapping tips about boys and clothes while I sat on the floor and played with the kittens and felt like a misfit. *This can't be happening*, I thought. *A misfit with my best friend here. This is so weird*.

Half an hour later, we were invited up to Leela's bedroom, where the conversation continued and Erin charmed Leela, Brook and Zahrah. We tried on clothes. We played music. Leela even put on a Bollywood movie and showed us how to do some of the dance steps. It was hysterical as the five of us danced down the stairs and into the kitchen, and even Auntie joined in for a few minutes.

When we left about an hour later, after a dish of Auntie's pistachio and coconut ice cream, Erin promised to call as soon as we could with a verdict about the kittens.

'Cool,' said Leela in an American accent. 'And don't be a stranger. Let's do lunch.'

Erin gave her an air kiss. 'OK. Have your people call my people,' she said in her fake USA drawl (which was awful).

Brook laughed. 'Crap accent,' she said in a friendly way as Leela closed the door.

The minute we were out of the driveway, Erin turned to me.

'India Jane Ruspoli, I can't believe it. You have been moaning on all term about being lonely and you've found it hard to make friends at your school, but those three are *extraterrestrial*. Why haven't you mentioned them or got in with them? Like, they're even in your year.'

I wanted to kill her. I wanted to kill her even more when I discovered that when I'd been out of the room for three minutes to use the loo, Leela'd invited Erin to a big family party there on Saturday night.

'Course I asked if I could bring you and they said OK,' she said as she Bollywood-danced along the street. 'Wow. I so love London already.'

My feet felt like lead. *Arghhhhhhhhhhhhhhhhhhh*, I thought as I trudged along behind her. *Argh. Argh. Arghhhhhhhhhhhh*.

Chapter 14

Prissy-knickers Pills

India Jane, said my inner Sensible Sadie, *you've got to cut this out. You're acting like a pathetic jealous sibling. Now GROW up.*

You're right, I thought. *That is, I'm right – because Sensible Sadie is me too, aren't you? Me? You're me. Oh whatever!*

I pulled my pillow out from underneath my head and sat up ready to lean over and bash Erin with it. She was always up for a good pillow fight when we had sleepovers back in Ireland, but the pull-out bed Mum had made up for her on the opposite side of my room was empty.

From downstairs came the sound of Dad's early-morning chanting. I was about to get up to close my bedroom door to shut it out when I realised that the *nam myoho renge kyo* had a distinctly female ring to it. *Oh no*, I thought as I scrambled out of bed, out into the hall and almost fell down the stairs.

When I reached the ground floor, I realised that my suspicions were right. There were Dad and Erin, both in their pyjamas and dressing gowns, cross-legged, eyes closed, chanting away. The room *reeked* of sandalwood incense and it looked as if instead of just lighting one joss stick to put by the fireplace, Dad had lit a whole packet. He never did anything in small measures.

Ohmigod, I thought as I closed the door to the front room and crept into the kitchen to make tea and toast. Ten minutes later, Dad and Erin came in to join me. They were both looking annoyingly smug and stank of joss sticks.

'India Jane doesn't approve,' said Dad as he took a piece of the toast I'd put on a plate in the middle of the table. 'Thinks my method is too noisy.'

'Me *and* the neighbours *and* Dylan *and* Kate *and* Aunt Sarah. The method I learned involved being quiet and going beyond noise, both internal and external.'

I immediately knew that I'd sounded like the Queen, and Erin and Dad both went, 'Ooooh,' and Erin pulled a silly face.

'India never was a morning person,' she said.

'It's the *inner* noise that one needs to quiet,' Dad started and then proceeded to drone on about meditation like I knew nothing about it, when it was *my* thing. *My thing.* The *one* thing I had done that no one else in the family did. I tried to catch Erin's eye so that we could have a giggle at him like we used to when he got on his high horse about something, but she was listening to him as if he was a blooming expert. Like the students in Greece used to look at Sensei.

'Er, I have already heard this, Dad,' I said. 'You seem to have forgotten that I studied with Sensei in Greece.'

'Oo-er, get her, Miss Know it All,' said Erin. 'We can't all swan off to islands in Greece to learn from a master you know.'

'Actually we can,' said Dad and he produced a leaflet from his dressing gown. 'Your man Sensei. He's doing a gig on Friday night in Chelsea.'

I rolled my eyes. 'Spiritual teachers don't do gigs, Dad.'

'You know what I mean,' said Dad. 'I picked up details on my way home from the arts centre. Want to go, Erin?'

'Ye*ah*, you betcha,' she said.

'What about me?' I asked.

'It's for newcomers,' said Dad. 'And . . . as you just told us, you've heard it all before.' For a second, he looked exactly like Dylan does when he has one over me. I felt like strangling him.

'B . . . but we were going to go and see a movie, Erin,' I protested.

Erin put on a snooty look. 'Ah yes, but one must tend to the needs of one's soul, don't you think, Mr Ruspoli?'

Dad nodded. 'Absolutissimo.'

They both cracked up laughing, high-fived each other, then proceeded to polish off my toast. It was blooming hard sometimes being a spiritual being when you lived with such *annoying* people.

'And course you can come with us,' said Dad. 'You could

do a refresher. You probably need it.'

'Thanks a bunch,' I said gloomily.

Seconds later, Dylan burst in and joined the conversation. He wanted to go and learn to meditate too.

'You're too young,' I said.

'Says who?' Dylan objected as Mum came in wearing her dressing gown. 'It's not illegal.'

'What's not illegal?' she asked as she put out cereal and bowls.

'Meditation,' Dylan replied. 'India Jane says I'm too young to do it.'

'Did she now?'

'Yeah. Just because she learned how to do it in Greece, she thinks she's the expert,' Dylan continued.

Mum shook her head as she got milk out of the fridge. 'But you don't practise it, do you, love? It's not enough to learn how to do it, you have to apply it every day otherwise it's like buying an exercise DVD but never doing it.'

'Or joining the gym and never going,' said Dad as he put more bread in the toaster.

'Really, India Jane?' said Erin. 'Don't you do it at all? I distinctly remember you saying just after you'd got back from Greece that, even though you'd found it hard sometimes, you were going to continue with it because it did make a difference, especially when you were stressed. You *did* say that, I remember. And you have been stressed lately, haven't you? So why haven't you been meditating?'

Grrrrr, I thought. *Grrrrr. GRRRRRR.* I had the distinct

feeling that I was being got at. Well and truly. Four faces were looking at me accusingly like I'd committed some humungous crime. 'Leave me alone! I *do* do it. Sometimes. In private. Just because I don't make a song and dance about it like Dad does and wake up the neighbourhood, doesn't mean I don't do it on my own.'

'Which means . . . she doesn't do it,' said Dylan and the others nodded in agreement, then everyone looked away as if they'd lost interest.

'If you don't mind, I've had rather a lot of things going on this term. I . . .'

'Excuses,' said Erin and tutted like an old lady before helping herself to cereal and fruit.

I looked over at her. 'You are supposed to be my friend,' I said.

'I am,' she said and beamed me a smile.

'Which means that you are supposed to be on my side.'

Erin shook her head. 'Not if I don't agree with you.'

The door opened and Kate drifted in to join us and she too listened as Dad, Erin and Dylan made plans for the meditation evening.

'Don't tell me you want to go too?' I asked. Kate had been very anti it all in Greece and I felt relieved when she shook her head.

'Can girls with boob jobs lie on their fronts? I don't think so. Me, meditate? Yeah, right,' she said, 'not my thing, but hey, Erin, if you want to hang out in the day, I could show you around a bit. And maybe later we could watch a DVD and paint each other's nails.'

I felt my mouth drop open. This was Kate. Cool Kate, who needed her space – and now she was offering to take Erin out and about. I felt the evil green snake raise its jealous head again.

'BUHwagoooooOOO,' I blurted.

Everyone burst out laughing.

'Anyone got a dictionary?' asked Erin. 'I know we both speak Shakespearian, but not sure what language that was. What are you trying to say, India?'

'Nothing,' I said. 'Just wrestling with one of my inner demons.'

'Aren't we all, dear?' said Dad and helped himself to *another* piece of toast.

And it *didn't* end there. Lewis came over later in the day and like the rest of them, was captivated. He and Erin had always got on and she'd had a crush on him since for ever. She immediately went all sheep-eyed over him, laughed at his terrible jokes, and sat with him on the sofa, eating popcorn and watching *Celebrity Makeovers*.

My friend, I thought as I watched through what felt like slit eyes from the opposite sofa. *Myyyyyy* friend.

Ethan and Jessica and the twins were over on the Thursday evening. *Hah*, I thought. *She won't win them over. The twins will get her. She won't stand for the ankle-biting.* But of course she did. She was down under the table with them, biting ankles, pretending to be dogs and Kate and Lewis thought it was *hilarious*.

What is happening? I asked myself as I looked on and felt like I'd taken a course of prissy-knickers pills. I loved her. Course I did. She was my best mate. She *was*. *So why*, I asked myself, *do I want her to go home?*

Chapter 15

Stake-out

'OK, so verily sweet lady, when do I meet yon gorgie-pie, Sir Joe of Notting Hill?' asked Erin. 'I am away on Sunday afternoon, 'tis already Friday and I haven't even set eyes on his fair features. Let's go and seeketh him out.'

'Noooooo. It's not like that,' I said. 'Erketh nonnie nay. I don't know him well enough. Oh *please* don't do an Erin and go and phone him up or anything. That would be so uncooleth and surely lead to calamity.'

Erin gave me her best disapproving look. 'Me? Uncooleth? As ifith! But we could put Planeth B into action.'

'Planeth B?'

'Yeah – I mean, yay. I take it that at least you know wherest he liveth? What walls dost encumbeth his manly limbs?'

I nodded. 'Yay, yay, and thrice times, yay. His mum helps run the centre in Greece so Aunt Sarah has her address in her book.'

Erin nodded. 'OK. So adorn thyself with jewels and lipeth-gloss and let's away. We're going to go and hang about outside his house and then when he comes out, we can accidentally-on-purpose bump into him.'

I shook my head. 'I don't think so, Erin. I think that might be a bit obvious.'

'Fie on thy doubt, oh fair maid. Course it's not obvi. I did it *loads* of times when I was into Scott. Oh come on, India, let's do a stake-out. I have to see him in the flesh to see if his hand art worthy of thine heart.'

'When thou dost speak such poetry, I cannot deny thee,' I said, so we tried on a few outfits (so we looked our best but casual), slicked on some lip-gloss, I put on some of the special cinnamon-based scent that Mum makes for me, Erin nicked a squirt of Aunt Sarah's Chanel No.19 from her bathroom, then we set off to spy on Joe's house. He lives on the opposite side of Holland Park and, as far as I knew from hearing Aunt Sarah talk about them, he has an older brother who was at university in Leeds so it was just Joe and his parents living at home. We found a tall terraced house with black railings at the front, a wrought-iron gate and steps down to what looked like a basement kitchen. Number 143. We strolled past a couple of times, then we positioned ourselves in an antique-shop doorway about a half a metre down the road, to survey the house. Five minutes went by. Ten. Fifteen.

The shop door opened. 'You girls want something or are you

just sheltering here?' asked an irate man with grizzly grey hair.

'We're admiring your shop window,' said Erin, doing her best to look innocent.

'For fifteen minutes? Yeah, right. On your way, sweetheart,' he said with a jerk of his thumb.

'Blooming cheek,' said Erin as we walked up the other way and positioned ourselves at a bus stop on the other side of Joe's house. Once again, nobody went in or came out.

'This is getting boring, isn't it?' asked Erin after a further ten minutes.

I nodded.

'We need to revert to Plan C,' she said.

I nodded. 'Just what is that?'

'Let me just take a peep inside the house.'

'No, Erin. Noooooooo.'

But she was off. She strolled up to the railings, then stood on the bottom rung and peered down into the basement.

'There's a light on,' she said as I raced up to her, grabbed her arm and tried to pull her away. 'Come on, Erin. Please don't do this. What if he's at home?'

As I pulled her away, she lost her balance slightly and her sunglasses fell off her head and down into the small area in front of the basement kitchen window. 'Oh noodles,' she said and opened the gate and began to scramble down.

'Eriiiiiin,' I said. 'What if someone's in there?'

'Be OK,' she called back. 'If they see us, they know you, so it's not as if they're going to think there's a burglar.'

'Well hurry up!' I said as I glanced up and down the street. Too late! Joe was cycling up the street. He saw me immediately, waved, and within seconds drew up beside me on the pavement.

'Just my blooming luck,' I muttered under my breath as I felt myself blush bright red.

'Hey, India,' he said. 'What you doing?'

'Oh. Just passing. My mate lost her sunglasses.'

Erin's face looked up by our ankles. 'Hiya,' she called and ran back up the steps to join us. Joe looked at us quizzically.

'Um. I didn't know you lived here,' I said as I pointed up at the house.

Joe burst out laughing. 'Here?' he asked.

I nodded. 'Yes. No idea at all. We just happened to be passing. Um. Yes. How are you?'

Joe was still laughing. 'OK. So if you didn't know I lived here, why did you just point to that house?'

'Oh . . .' I started as I realised that I'd just totally blown it.

Erin began to laugh too. 'Good point, Joe.'

Joe smiled. 'And how do you know who I am?' he asked.

'She doesn't,' I said. 'Oh bollards. Joe, this is my mate, Erin. Erin, this is Joe.'

Erin gave Joe a sweet smile. 'Oh, so *you're* Joe. India has told me so much about you.'

I. Could. Not. Believe. It. *Why not complete my humiliation and give him copies of the emails I sent you, Erin*, I thought. *The ones that say 'I think I've found my soul mate'*.

Joe's eyes filled with amusement. 'Has she now? Hi, Erin. I

162

think she's mentioned you too. So, India. You're quite right. I do live here. Er . . . good guess or not. Want to come in?'

Erin nodded while I said something in Hogwashese. It sounded like, 'Merahuhna'.

Joe looked for his keys, then opened the front door and wheeled his bike in. Erin leaned over to me and whispered, 'Totally totally gorgeous – and those eyelashes? Divine.'

Joe led us through the narrow hall, past stairs into a square country-type kitchen at the back with an Aga and shelves lined with pulses and seeds and dried fruits. It smelled of apples and toast. He made us drinks, then he and Erin chatted away about art and the school play and London.

'And I'm going to learn to meditate this evening,' she said.

'Yeah. India did that in Greece, didn't you?'

I nodded. I seemed to have lost my tongue. *Why, oh why, can't I be Miss Cool, the way I am with Callum?* I asked myself.

For a moment, Joe turned his back to get something and Erin kicked me and made a jerky movement with her chin. I knew what she was trying to say and that was – speak up, you eejit! I held up my hands and shrugged as if to say – it's hopeless. Erin glared at me, so I made my eyes go crossed and mock-strangled myself – just as Joe turned around. He looked as if he was having a hard time not laughing again. 'Er . . . you OK, India Jane?' he asked.

I nodded.

'My friend seems to be having a bonkers attack this afternoon,' said Erin. 'I think aliens have captured her and eaten her brain.'

'Oh that,' said Joe. 'Yes. It happens a lot around here. Er . . . yeah, hope you feel better soon. Can be nasty, that — aliens eating your brain. I hope it didn't hurt *too* much.'

Erin creased up laughing. 'Hmm,' she said. 'Cute *and* funny.'

She was *flirting* with Joe . . . Joe. *My* Joe. And he looked pleased at what she'd said. *Oh God, can this week get any worse? Please, please God, don't let Joe fall in love with Erin.*

Quick, India Jane, said my inner Sensible Sadie, *say something flirty too. Stay in the game. Stay in the game.*

'Glurp,' I said, and Erin and Joe both stared at me. 'Glurp. Yes. That means "funny" in Hogwashese, which is my special language, so you are cute and glurpy. And in case you were wondering if I spoke any other languages, I do. Shakespearian.'

Behind Joe, Erin made a despairing face and a sign to say she was shooting herself, while Joe looked at me as if I was totally bonkers. And then I got an attack of the giggles and my shoulders started shaking and I couldn't stop laughing. After a short while, Erin began too.

Joe looked from me to Erin and back again, then shook his head. 'I will never, ever, *ever* understand girls,' he said, but he didn't look upset about it, which was a relief.

We left Joe's about half an hour later and, as soon as we were a short distance away, Erin grabbed my arm. 'He sooooo fancies you.'

'Me? It was you who was being Miss Flirty McGirty. He fancied you.'

Erin shook her head. 'Oh nooooo. You, my dear. It's just a

164

matter of time. Although . . . it might help if you stopped talking hogwash when he's around.'

'I know. Can't help it,' I said and suddenly I felt ridiculously happy. Erin thought that Joe fancied me. And Erin usually knows about these things. 'Why? Why do you think he fancies me?'

Erin rolled her eyes. 'It's obvi. Did you not see the look on your man's face when he saw you and the way he looks at you really tenderly whenever you say something stupid – which is often.'

'I thought that look was pity. He does it a lot. Looks at me like he's having a hard time not laughing at me.'

'Not at you. Like you amuse him, and that's different and that's what gives him away. Oh yes, it's just a matter of time.'

We carried on down the road, stopping to look in the occasional shop window, reliving the meeting with Joe and laughing our heads off. *This is what it's like to have a mate around*, I thought as we bought Liquorice All Sorts from the newsagent's and stuffed our faces with them.

'So these new friends of yours,' said Erin as she popped an All Sort into her mouth. 'Aren't they back today?'

I nodded. Actually, Ruby was supposed to have been back the night before and Nicole the day before that. What I didn't tell her was that I was hurt that neither of them had called to say that they were home or even texted from their holiday homes. I'd told myself that they'd been too busy, but then so had I, and *I'd* made the time to text at the beginning of the week. But only the once. When I didn't get a reply from either of them, I decided to leave it. I didn't want to appear desperate or clingy or needy. All the same, it hurt. I knew that real mates phoned as soon as they got back from being away and even texted on the way to the airport and as soon as they got off the plane when they came back.

Being with Erin for the week had reminded me what friendship was all about. Despite my blip of jealousy, it had been a great week with her. We had explored loads of London that I didn't know. We'd hung out in Hampstead, cruised Camden Lock, perused Portobello Market, been down the King's Road and into TopShop in Oxford Street where we'd both bought fab outfits from the latest collection for Leela's party. It had been great to have someone to do it all with, to try stuff on with and then sit and people-watch.

However, being with her had also made me aware of what a failure I'd been at making new mates and I was beginning to wonder if it was my fault – if there was something wrong with me. I felt like I was going through a whole crisis to do with friendship and didn't know if it was my fault and my expectations were too high or *what* the problem was. Even Mikey seemed to have moved on since he'd met his girlfriend. He was away in Cornwall for half-term and he hadn't texted either. The only person who had been in touch was Callum – he'd left a message on my voicemail saying he was looking forward to resuming rehearsals when we were back at school. I'd texted him back to be polite, but I decided to call it a day with him. It wasn't going to go anywhere. Months ago, I would have blurted this all out to Erin, but now I felt myself holding back. I was becoming Paranoid Penny and I didn't want her to think that I was a saddo or a loser and maybe go back to Ireland wondering if she still wanted to be my mate. Maybe I'd got boring. And weird. Or too demanding. Or too introspective. And self-obsessed. Or was I normal? I didn't know any more.

When we got back home and were about to go inside the front door, my phone rang.

'Hi,' I said and mouthed to Erin that it was Ruby while I found my door key and let us both in. Erin nodded that she understood and walked inside. I felt relieved that Ruby had phoned when she did, so that Erin could see that I *did* have some friends after all. I wasn't a total Molly No Mates. Ruby was in usual Ruby-mode and after giving me the low down on her holiday, asked if I could go over that evening.

'But my friend from Ireland is here and we're going to a meeting about meditation.'

'Bring her with you.'

'No. She *wants* to go to the meeting.'

'OK, so let her go.'

'But I said I'd go too.'

'But hasn't she been there all week?'

'Yeah.'

'So you've had loads of time with her. Isn't there anyone else going to the meeting, which by the way, I have to say sounds deadly dull. Like, isn't meditation for wacko-jobs?'

'Dad's going and my brother, and no, it isn't for wackos. I used to think that but actually —'

'Whatever. So loads of people are going and I'm ALL on my own. Oh come on, India, be a mate. Come over.'

I felt torn. Erin would be going back on Sunday and it was true, Dad and Dylan *were* going to the meeting whereas Ruby was a new mate, part of my new life, and if I didn't have her and Nicole to hang out with at school, I'd have nobody.

'Oh, I don't know, Ruby . . .'

'Pleeeeeeeeese, pleeeeeese.'

'What about Nicole? Isn't she back?'

'Yeah. She's been back for days, but she has some family thing today. I've left *so* many messages for her but she's obviously got more important things to do. Pleeeeese, India, I'm going to be all on my ownsome and I need to talk to you about loads of stuff. It's really important and you're the only one who understands and gives me good advice.'

Erin was watching me and I pulled a face and pointed at the phone. 'Let me talk to Erin and I'll call you back, OK?'

'Please, please. And I'm sure if Erin is a *real* mate, she'll understand. So see you later?'

'Later.'

When I'd hung up, I realised that as usual she hadn't asked a thing about how my week had been or what I'd been doing. Or even considered for a moment that I might actually like to go the meeting with Sensei. But that was Ruby.

'Ruby,' I said to Erin. 'She's back. Wants me to go over.'

'I heard. That's nice but . . . is she always like that?'

'Like what?'

'Sounds like she likes to get her way.'

'Yeah. No. Not really. She's fun. You'd like her.'

'Did she ask to meet me?'

'Er . . . not exactly . . . She said I could bring you along.'

Erin raised an eyebrow. 'So what did she want?'

'Me to go over to her place.'

'Does she ever come here?'

'Not really. Or that is, she came once when she wanted to talk about something. Er . . . she prefers to meet up at her house and I don't really mind going there. She lives in an amazing place.'

Erin raised her other eyebrow. 'So do you. I heard you saying about the meeting, but if you'd prefer to go and see her, do go. I'll be fine with your dad and Dylan and I know that you've heard it all before – about the meditation, that is.'

'I would like to come with you. I really would. I liked listening to Sensei in Greece and I did say I already had plans this evening.'

'I know. So why didn't you say no to Ruby?'

'Hard to get a word in sometimes.'

Erin nodded. 'I heard.'

'And . . . oh God, this is awkward, but . . . well you're going to be gone soon, and Ruby and Nicole, well, they're my new mates – it's early days still and I . . . well, I want them to like me.'

Erin nodded. 'Sure. Sure,' she said. 'You'd better go, although

169

I can't imagine who wouldn't ever like you. But you go, sounds to me like you've been summoned.'

I quickly called Ruby back and said that I'd be there later. After I'd put the phone down, I made an effort to laugh. 'I suppose Ruby is a bit of a teen queen. But she's OK, a what-you-see-is-what-get-type of person.'

Erin linked my arm and looked right into my eyes. 'I just want you to be happy, India Jane. Are you?'

'Yeah. Yeah, I am,' I said, but for some reason, all of a sudden, I felt like crying.

An hour later, Mum, Dad, Dylan and Erin set off for Sensei's meeting. Just before they left, I apologised to Erin.

'I feel weird about this,' I said.

She gave me a hug. 'No need. I understand. Ruby and the other girl are your new mates. Why should they want to meet me? And you have to work at friendships. You're right.'

'*We* don't have to work very hard,' I said.

Erin made her face go straight. 'I do,' she said wearily, then cracked up. 'Ah but we don't have to work at it because I am Queen Fab Friend. You know that.'

I laughed. 'Queen Fab Friend and modest too.'

'*So* modest,' said Erin as Dad hurried her and Dylan out of the door. 'Have a great evening.'

When the door had closed and I was alone in the hall, I picked up the phone to call Ruby and let her know that I was on my way over.

Her mum picked up the phone. 'Ruby? She's not here, dear. She went out over an hour ago.'

'Oh! Is she coming back soon? She called earlier to ask me over.'

'*Did* she? Are you sure? She never said anything to me about anyone coming over and I'm certain that she won't be back this evening. She's gone to stay with her friend Nicole. Maybe you got the wrong night?'

I knew I hadn't got the wrong night. Ruby had got a better offer and not bothered to let me know. 'Yes. Of course. The wrong date. Sorry.'

'That's all right. Who shall I say called?'

'No one,' I said. 'It doesn't matter. I'll see her at school.'

I put the phone down. I had Ruby's mobile now and could have phoned her but there didn't seem to be any point. My eyes filled up with the tears that had been threatening all afternoon. How was I going to explain this to Erin and the rest of them when they arrived back, full of shining light and bliss?

Chapter 16

New Friends

'Oh hi, India, it's Leela.'

'Oh hi,' I replied in what I hoped was a bright voice so that she wouldn't realise that I had spent the last half hour blubbing for Britain. After the call to Ruby's house, it was like a dam had broken inside of me and I couldn't stop.

'Listen, I'm phoning for a humungous favour.'

'OK.'

'Well, you know we're having this party tomorrow night?'

'Yeah?'

'Mum's worried that the kittens'll get freaked out . . . Hey, you OK? You sound like you've got a cold?'

'Yeah. No. Um, hayfever,' I said as I blew my nose.

'In October?'

'I'm allergic to . . . um, autumn . . . er, leaves.'

Leela laughed at the other end of the phone. 'Leaves? Okaaaaay. So, thing is, Mum wanted to know if you would mind looking after the kittens for a day or so, while our house is full of people. Could you do that?'

I hesitated for only a second. 'Absolutely. Hundred per cent. Love to.'

'Cool. Mum said she thought you would because she could see that you were an animal lover.'

'But I can't get them tonight because everyone's out and —'

'Where?'

'Meditation meeting.'

'Why didn't you go?'

'I was going to. I know the teacher from Greece.'

'Oh Sensei. Yeah. My sister's into him.'

'Anisha. Yeah I know.'

'So why didn't you go with them?'

'I . . . oh long story, complicated.'

'You sure you're OK, India? You sound sort of . . . bunged up.'

'Yeah. I'm fine. Really.'

'If you say so. OK. I'll get my brother, Rajiv, to drop me round. There's just the two of them. We'll bring everything they need.'

'I thought there were three.'

'One of the girls has gone. Someone Mum works with at the pharmacy took her. So it's just two. Is that OK?'

'Deffo,' I said.

'See you in half an hour.'

I ran to the bathroom, splashed my face with cold water and

173

put some make-up on. I even thought of wearing sunglasses because my eyes were so puffy, but decided that might look a bit weird seeing as it was dark outside. True to her word, thirty minutes later Leela arrived. She seemed in a hurry and thrust a cat litter tray at me and a bag of food and litter.

'Can't stay, million things to do but . . .' She scrutinised my eyes. 'You OK?'

'Yeah. It's some kind of weird allergy. Makes my eyes puffy.'

'Okaaaay,' she said, but she looked doubtful. Outside a car honked. 'That's Rajiv. Everything's mad at home getting ready for the do and Mum's gone into sergeant-major mode and given us all a list of things to do. So. The kittens are in this basket. They've been fed. They know how to use the litter tray and . . . Erin here?'

'No. Still out with Dad and everyone.'

The car outside honked again. 'OK. Laters. Any probs, call me, yeah?' she turned to go. 'Hey, you are coming tomorrow, aren't you?'

I nodded. 'If that's OK?'

'Course it is. Why wouldn't it be? Be nice to hang out and there's a few people coming from school. Oh and Anisha will be back. You said you knew her, yeah?'

'Yeah.'

And then she was gone. I got a feeling that she knew that I was upset. I remembered something that Erin had said once about how real friends listened not only to what you say, but also what you didn't say. Leela struck me as the kind of girl who could do that and, once again, I wished that she was my friend.

I put the basket down, knelt beside it and opened the lid. Two worried faces peeped out and looked around. Both of them seemed hesitant to get out, so I stroked their heads. I so knew how they were feeling. Starting over in a strange place. They must have been wondering what the heck was happening to them. 'Oh sweeties, it's going to be OK,' I said. 'I know this is all new but I'm going to look after you and we're all going to be the best of friends, for a very, *very* long time.'

Now all I have to do is convince Aunt Sarah the same, I thought as the boy kitten clambered out and came to sit on my knee.

'Yin and Yang,' said Dad.

'Mars and Venus,' said Dylan.

'India should name them,' said Erin. 'She's the one who saw the notice.'

The kittens were an instant hit. As soon as everyone got back from the meditation meeting, they were the centre of attention and passed from one knee to the other. The girl didn't seem to mind and was soon purring away, but the boy kitten went and hid under the sofa at first at the first opportunity.

'They know when they're in a safe place,' said Mum. 'He'll come out in his own time, especially when he realises that we have the cat food.'

'Do you think we'll be able to keep them?' I asked.

'Absolutely,' said Mum. 'And if Sarah objects, we'll hide them in the cellar for a day or so and think of some way we can blackmail her. I must have some dirt on her from when we were young. Call Mrs Ranjani and tell her that we'd like to keep them.'

I laughed at the glimpse of how Mum must have been when she was a young disobedient girl. When everyone was distracted with the cats, I nipped out into the hall, got the portable phone and took it into the kitchen where I had some privacy. I dialled Ruby's mobile. She picked up almost immediately.

'Hi Ruby, it's India Jane,' I blurted before I chickened out.

There was a moment's hesitation. 'Oh, hi, India.'

'Hi. Remember when you called this afternoon you asked me over and I said I'd come?'

'Um, er . . . yeah but —'

'I'd just like to remind you that I cancelled my plans with my friends and family, and by the time I found out that you'd gone out and not bothered to let me know, it was too late for me to go to the meeting with the others like I wanted to.'

Again there was silence for a few moments. 'Er yeah, um, something came up.'

'I realise that,' I said. 'I don't need to know what, or hear excuses, I just think that you could have had the decency to let me know. A call would have taken less than a minute. My evening was ruined because you didn't bother —'

'No need to get upset about it,' said Ruby.

'You know what? I'm not upset. Not any more. I was. But it made me realise something about friendship. It's about respect as well as other things. Respect that other people's time and their feelings are valuable as yours.'

And then I hung up. I was shaking slightly as I hate confrontation, but I felt good for having said what I'd said and I realised that as much as friends needed to respect each other, I needed to respect myself and not let anyone treat me like a convenience until a better offer came along.

I went back to join the others, and at bedtime took the kittens up to my room as I didn't want to leave them on their own in the dark in a strange house on their first night. Even though the boy was still nervous and went under the bed as soon as I put him down on the floor, later when everything went quiet, he crawled out to look for his sister. I went to sleep that night with them both curled up on the end of my bed, both with their paws around each other.

'Totally adorable,' I said.

'And so is Leela's brother,' said Erin. 'I can't wait to meet him in the flesh tomorrow night.'

As I drifted off to sleep, at last I felt that my list of what I wanted in a friend was becoming clear:

Someone who's around at the weekends and in the hols.

Someone I can be totally myself with and who can be herself with me.

Someone to laugh and cry with — there on good and bad days.

Someone I can trust with my secrets.

Someone who will be honest with me (even if it hurts).

Someone who is glad when good things happen to me — who isn't in competition or jealous when something nice happens to me.

Someone who puts friends first before boys.

An equal relationship with a balance of talking and listening.

Someone who doesn't only call when in need or to dump their stuff on me.

Someone who doesn't try to control me.

ZZZzzzzzzzzzzzzz.

Chapter 17

Party Time

The evening of the party came round so fast, and as I got ready, I had mixed feelings – looking forward to it as I liked parties and I'd be with Erin, but also sad because it was our last night together. Erin had been out with Dad in the afternoon to see Sensei again and had learned to do the same meditation as I had. She had come back eager to give it a go, and made me laugh because I went to have a bath while she meditated and when I came back, she was slumped on the floor, fast asleep.

'Some things haven't changed since Ireland,' I said. We'd tried to meditate from a book once years ago and she'd fallen asleep then.

'Early days,' she said as she sat up and rubbed her eyes. 'And you found it hard in the beginning.'

'Still do. Sometimes it's easier than others. Like some days, your mind is all over the place and other days, it's really easy to focus. Either way, it makes you feel better – like doing it recharges the batteries.'

'And a little nap in the day can't hurt either, though I'll try to stay awake while I do it in the future,' said Erin and went to the wardrobe to pull out our new outfits. (I'd got a fitted pearl-grey Victorian-style jacket with short collar. It had ruffle details on the side and neck and tiny military buttons down the front. I was going to wear it with my jeans and grey stripey Converse All Stars. Erin's dress was pure Hollywood and was black pleated chiffon with one shoulder strap.) 'Now. To more important matters. What jewels to wear and what are we going to do about you getting off with Joe?'

'Getting off with Joe? Nothing,' I replied. 'And I mean it.'

'Ooh. Miss Strict. I just think that sometimes you have to make things happen.'

'No, Erin. No. And if you do, I will kill you.'

'OK. But you need to snog him soon or some other girl will get in there. Boys like him don't stay single for very long. You need to seal the deal with a kiss and then he will never be able to forget you.'

'Yeah, sure. We don't even know that he's going to be there.'

'Why not? Think about it. Joe's mum works with your aunt and Anisha, so they all know each other, so chances are Joe will have had an invite.'

'Maybe.' I put an extra slick of lip-gloss on just in case.

★ ★ ★

Dad dropped us at the house, where a boy of Dylan's age was acting as usher and guided us by torchlight down the side of the house and into a huge marquee that had been put up in the back garden.

'Yum,' said Erin as we were both hit with the fabulous aroma of Indian cooking. It looked fabulous and a long buffet table to the left was groaning with enough food to feed an army. Seats were set out around the edge of the marquee, but most people were standing and chatting. To the right, in the corner, a disco had been set up, but the music that came out of the speakers angled in each corner of the marquee was gentle sitar-playing.

'Ah. Now is the winter of our disco tent,' I said as I looked around and did a quick burst of disco dancing.

Erin cracked up. That was the great thing about having such a close mate, she immediately got the reference to the *Now is the winter of our discontent* line in Shakespeare's *Richard III*. Anyone else would think we were talking nonsense, but we got each other's sense of humour. Suddenly she nudged me and I looked over to where she was staring. There was Joe. 'Told you he'd be here,' she said as he waved and came straight over.

'Hi,' he said. 'Been guessing where people don't live again?'

'Very funny,' I said. 'I blame Erin. She's always getting me into trouble.'

Erin grinned. 'So, India Jane. Would you like a drink?'

'Yeah. I'll come with you.'

'Noooooooooooooooooooo. Oh no. I can manage. Er, stay here with Joe. Yes, Joe. What can I get you?'

Joe indicated that he had a can of lager in his hand.

'Oh yes,' she said. 'OK. I'll be off then. Now play nice, children.'

She walked off a few steps then turned around and, behind Joe's back, made a smooching face and held her heart. I ignored her in the same way that I ignore Dylan when he does the same stupid thing.

'So, how's it going?' Joe asked. 'Good half-term?'

'Yeah, it's been great having Erin to stay. You?'

'Yeah. You know. Got a theme for the play yet?'

'Nah. Don't remind me.'

For a few moments, we stood in silence. Joe took a sip of his lager. I looked around the room and searched my mind for something to say. I remembered what Erin had said about boys like him not being single for long and wondered if he was still unattached or was with someone again.

'So. Got back with Mia?' I blurted, then clapped my hand over my mouth. I hadn't meant to actually voice what I was thinking. 'Oh sorry. None of my business. Sometimes things just come out . . .'

Joe smiled. 'I'd noticed.' And he looked into my eyes and there was that vibe again. The vibe that made me feel like warm honey was flooding through me.

'Oh . . . I . . . Oh God. Sorry. Sometimes I just talk rubbish.'

'Hogwashese,' said Joe with a smile. 'I'm thinking of taking lessons so I can understand you. Actually Mia is with someone else now, so that's cool. Some guy in his first year at university.'

182

He was still looking at me in a way that made my toes curl up. 'And you? Still with Callum?'

'Nah,' I said. 'There are already two people in that relationship. Him and him.' Joe cracked up, so I decided to take a risk and moved in a tiny bit further. 'So that leaves you and me both single.'

Joe leaned in and I swear for a moment that he was going to kiss me. I began to close my eyes in anticipation. The party was getting off to a great start. Suddenly Joe pulled back and shook his head.

'No. Nope. Can't do this.'

'Whu . . .? Why not? Can't do what?'

Joe pointed at me and then at himself. 'Me. You. You know. Us.'

All my inner voices got together and growled in frustration. *Grrrrrrrrrrrrrrrrrrr.* 'Why not?'

Joe took a deep breath. 'I promised myself I wouldn't.' He looked around the room as if looking for escape.

'Don't worry, I'm not going to pounce but . . . I'd like to know *why* you promised yourself you wouldn't.'

Joe looked pleadingly at me. 'It's not that I don't like you, India. I do. You know I do, it's . . .'

So he *did* fancy me! My inner girls were doing cartwheels and singing hallelujah.

'It's *what*?' I asked.

'Too close to home,' he groaned.

'No you're not. You live on the other side of the park.'

'Not geographically, India. Just . . .'

'What? If you don't tell me I will have to kill you, or get my three brothers *and* my dad to come and beat you up.'

Joe smiled, reached out and took my hand. 'Remember I told you what I was like, on the plane. That I haven't exactly been Mr Commitment in my life, not with anyone, and I know I hurt some people, and before Greece I'd decided I wanted to change.'

'I remember,' I said. I remembered every second of the plane journey home. Sitting next to him, our thighs touching, having to resist not leaning over and nibbling his bottom lip . . .

'That's why I tried to make a go of it with Mia,' he continued. 'Then I met you and there you were in Greece . . . but I didn't want to do it again . . .' He went quiet and stared moodily across the room.

'Do what again? Oh. I see. Cheat on Mia.'

'Yeah. And I didn't, did I? I was determined not to cheat, which is why I . . . kind of kept out of your way. Nothing happened with us.'

It felt amazing to finally hear his side of the story and know that he had felt what I'd felt. 'No. It didn't. But there was a vibe.'

Joe looked at me again and I felt electricity zap through me from my head to my toes. 'Still is,' he said.

It was taking everything I had not to lean in and kiss him. 'But now you're single. You wouldn't be cheating on anyone.'

Joe sighed. 'Ah. But what if I did. Not now. Maybe not in a week, but I know what I'm like, and say a few months down the line, if I hurt you . . . well, this is where the close-to-home bit comes in. We not only go to the same school, but your aunt is my mum's best friend.'

'And that's it? That's why you won't let yourself get too close to me?'

Joe nodded and his eyes looked sad. 'Yeah. But we can be friends, yeah?'

'Pathetic, Donahue. That is the biggest pile of crap I've ever heard.'

Joe's eyes widened in surprise. 'Really?'

'Yeah, really. Total bollards.' And I leaned in, looked into his eyes for a second so that we could both feel the heat, and then I kissed him. In a nano-second, he began to kiss me back. A long deep kiss. It was *totally* extraterrestrial. When we finally pulled back, he looked at me and smiled.

'I've been wanting to do that for a very long time,' he said.

'Me too,' I said. 'But we're going to be friends, yeah?' I turned away. 'So, laters.'

As I began to walk off, I heard him laugh softly. 'India Jane Ruspoli, you are going to do my head in.'

I turned back. 'Oh I do hope so,' I said, then went off to find Erin.

Erin was at the drinks table. 'Yabadabadabado,' I said as I punched the air. 'I managed to be cool, flirt, snog and leave him wanting more.'

Erin put her palms together and bowed. 'Excellent. You are

learning the ways of the seductress well, O India Jane Skywalker. You must let the Force be with you and boys can not resist.'

'Indeed, let the Force be with us and let's follow the yellow-brick road too while we're at it.'

At that moment, I noticed on the other side of the room that Nicole and Ruby had arrived. They walked in and stopped at the entrance as though they had been announced. They looked around so that people could register that they had arrived and then, with a flick of the hair, they both sashayed into the marquee as if strutting down a catwalk.

Erin raised an eyebrow. 'Quite an entrance,' she said. 'Who are those two?'

All the elation that I'd felt only seconds ago deflated like balloon letting out its air. 'Yeah, quite an entrance. That's Ruby and Nicole.'

'Oh,' said Erin.

'Oh,' I said.

'And you didn't know they were coming?'

'No, but then . . . I guess I didn't tell them that I was coming either.'

'Yeah, like Ruby didn't let you know that she was going out last night after you'd put off your plans with me for her. *Grrrr*,' said Erin and she put her arm around me.

'Oh don't worry, I called and let her know what I thought of that.'

Erin looked at me approvingly. 'Did you? Good. Because if

you hadn't said something, I would have. So let's go and let them know that you're here.'

'No. No. It's fine. I can fight my own battles and I said what I needed to say last night. I don't want the party to be ruined because of bad feeling between us.'

I was about to turn away, but Nicole had spotted me and said something to Ruby, who looked over. She looked surprised to see me and for a nano-second looked a little awkward, but immediately masked it with a big smile. She pulled on Nicole's arm and the two of them came over.

'Hiya,' they both said.

'Hi,' I said and introduced them to Erin.

'Hi,' said Erin very coolly. 'India has told me so much about you, all bad, hahahaha.'

Nicole looked closely at Erin as if she wasn't quite sure how to take her. Erin kept her expression a mask of indifference.

Ruby went into flattery mode. 'So how are you? And don't you both look lovely.'

'And so do you,' said Erin in exactly the same tone and the two girls looked at each other with pure hate. *Oops*, I thought.

'So. How naff is this?' said Nicole as she and Ruby took a plastic cup of cranberry juice that a passing waiter handed her. 'I mean they can't even afford real cups.'

'Oh I'm sure they can,' I said. 'Leela's parents own three pharmacies. I think they're being very sensible as it wouldn't be practical to use the best crystal in a garden, would it? Broken glass and all that.'

'Suppose,' said Nicole, then she proceeded to do her run down on everyone present, laughing at what people were wearing and criticising who was with who. She didn't seem to notice that Erin and I weren't laughing.

Suddenly Ruby looked behind us. 'Stop everything. I have just seen the love of my life. Ohmigod. Who is he?'

We looked over to where she was looking and saw that Rajiv had come in and gone over to the disco area, where he was talking to the DJ.

'Oh that's Leela's brother, Rajiv,' I said. 'Would you like me to introduce you?' To my right, I could tell that Erin was having a hard time not laughing.

'Absolutely,' said Ruby, 'he's lush.' She turned in her usual flamboyant manner, but as she did, *whoosh*, she'd slopped her cranberry juice all over Erin.

Erin leaped back and so did Nicole and so did I.

'Ohmigod,' gushed Ruby. 'Oh I'm soooooo sorry. Let me get you a cloth. Oh God. Thank God your dress is black, Erica.'

'Erin,' I said. 'E. R. I. N.'

But Ruby didn't look that sorry and I swear that Nicole was having trouble holding back a snigger. I felt as if I was seeing them in a totally new light. *How come I hadn't noticed before how bitchy they can be?* I asked myself.

'It's OK,' said Erin, 'but oh no, India, it's splashed your lovely jacket and that does show.'

I glanced down. There was a great red stain on the sleeve. 'Oh noooo,' I said.

Ruby looked down too. 'It will be OK. I'll pay for your dry-cleaning and you look so fab in it no one's going to notice a little stain. Oh God, I'm so clumsy.'

'It's OK,' I said. 'I am *sure* you didn't mean to do it on purpose.'

Erin shot Ruby a filthy look. 'Come on, India, let's go and find a loo where we can sponge it off while it's still wet.'

Ruby looked at Nicole and shrugged as if to say, What can I do? Nicole raised an eyebrow as if in agreement.

When we got to the bathroom, I took the jacket off and Erin did what she could to soak it.

'India. I totally forbid you to be friends with those girls,' she said.

'Yeah I —'

'Ruby's patronising and uses you to dump on when no one else will listen to her, like last night, and Nicole is just mean. Don't you see how insecure she is? That's why she feels she has to run everyone at the party down. It makes her feel big.'

'I know. I was coming to that conclusion myself, but they were the only people I had to hang out with and they're not so bad really. A bit self-centred, that's all. If I hadn't spent time with them, there was no one else. You don't know what it's been like. I did try, you know.'

Erin put her arm around me. 'I am sure you have. But you deserve friends who are worthy of you.'

'Worthy of me? I —'

'Yeah. Of you. You're one of the best people I know and

anyone should be glad to have you as a friend. You're funny and kind and thoughtful and if they haven't got the decency to call you over the half-term or let you know that they were coming to the party too and see if you wanted to come along with them, then dump them because they really aren't your true friends. Friends are there for each other.'

She looked so earnest, I couldn't help but smile. 'I guess. I think I —'

'You've been there for them, haven't you?'

'Yeah. I think friends are important and I —'

'So why shouldn't you expect the same in return? You're not asking for anything that you're not prepared to give. And you give a lot. It has to be two-way to work. Don't give yourself away to people who don't appreciate you.'

'I won't, Erin. You are right, and you know what? I did lose my confidence for a while back there, I was even worried that you wouldn't want to be my mate any more if I told you what a sad loser I've been. A real Molly No Mates. But I —'

'You are so not a sad loser. And I will always be your mate. Through thick and thin. Forever. You don't want fair-weather friends who are only there when things are good; real friends are there through it all. Real friends witness your life. Your whole life. Good times. Crap times. I'll be there for you and I hope you'll be there for me and be someone I can call when life is rubbish and I feel the whole world is against me, and someone I can share the glory days with when I'm a winner and everything's going my way.'

'The ups and downs,' I said and then I laughed. 'I feel a song coming on.'

Erin slapped my arm. 'I'm being serious. I've come over all Wise Woman of Wombatland.'

'I know . . . and I appreciate it and what I've been trying to say for the last five minutes is that I agree. It's taken me a while, but last night when Ruby just breezed off without a thought about letting me know, it sealed the deal for me. Or rather no deal. I don't want, or, as you say, deserve, friends like that. Like them. I want real mates or nothing and I'm not going to settle for second best and OK, so it may take a while, but I can wait.'

'Good,' said Erin.

'Good.'

'I know I've got the old crowd over in Ireland, but I do miss you, you know, it's not been the same since you left.'

'I miss you too. So much.'

'Group hug,' said Erin and made her eyes go crossed.

We looked at each other, shook our heads and chorused. 'Nah.'

And then we hugged.

I really do love Erin.

For the rest of the party, we kept out of Ruby and Nicole's way, and when Ruby saw Erin dancing with Rajiv, I noticed them leave about ten minutes later. I played it cool with Joe and although I could see him checking out where I was, I decided that my plan of action was to be elusive. I could tell he needed some space, but I was glad that I had kissed him as it had let me know that I hadn't imagined that there was definitely something between us. Mikey turned up with his girlfriend, Megan, halfway through the party so I had them to chat with while Erin was with Rajiv. After everyone had eaten and danced a little, suddenly the lights in the marquee went down.

Leela's mum got up on to the stage and went to the microphone and thanked everyone for coming. 'And to finish the party, we'd like to give you a little entertainment. I hope you enjoy it.'

The lights came on again, some sitar music began to play and then blasted out into Bollywood rock music that got everyone's feet tapping. From the opening of the tent, ten women dressed in red-and-gold saris appeared, then danced into the room. They looked wonderful with their dark kohl-smudged eyes and jewels glittering in their hair. Soon they were joined by ten men in three-quarter-length kaftan coats over Indian trousers. Their dancing was superb and towards the end of the routine, from somewhere on the roof of the marquee, glitter was released so that it looked like it was raining diamonds. The dancers pulled everyone on to the dance floor and the place erupted, with people's arms waving, everyone trying to Indian dance with everything they'd got. Erin and I were immediately up doing the moves that Leela and her friends had shown us earlier in the week. As I watched the spectacle of colour and sound, I suddenly had an idea. Over the other side of the room, Joe was dancing about like a madman. I danced Indian-style over to him.

'So what do you think?' I asked.

'Brilliant. Great,' he said and put his arm around my waist and spun me round.

I indicated the whole marquee with my arms. 'So. Bollywood. For the play.'

'For the play?' he asked and then the penny dropped. '*Yeah*. Bollywood! Bollytastic.'

'That's what I thought,' I said. 'I'm going to call Barry right now.'

Chapter 18

Starting Over – Again

Cinnamongirl: Parting isn't sweet sorrow, fie on that line, O Willie of Stratford, for thou dost speak with a forked tongue. Indeed, there's nothing sweet about parting, verily it sucketh and doth taste like a foul thing, for my heart doth feel like lead and I doth mith you. Oops, gone into lisp speak!

Irishbrat4eva: Lispeth not, fair friend, for though sea and sky may keep us apart, we have the bond of friendship for ever and a day.

Cinnamongirl: For ever.

Irishbrat4eva: Indeedie dododee. For ever. And now I must away for my repast, for yon matriach of the house doth yelleth up the stairs. I bid thee goodbye til it be morrow.

Cinnamongirl: Farewell fair —

'You OK?' Dad asked as he came into my bedroom as I was finishing on the computer to Erin. She'd only been back home in Ireland about fifteen minutes, but already had been in touch. *Thank God for MSN*, I thought as I closed down the computer and wondered how people managed in past times. Pigeon-carrier? Post? It would be awful to have to wait for days for a letter. Being able to talk to Erin so immediately made me feel that she hadn't completely disappeared from my life.

I nodded to Dad, but I didn't feel OK. I felt sad. I'd been curled up on my bed with the laptop balanced on my stomach and my new best friends, the kittens, Posh and Becks – so named because the boy kitten liked to play footie with anything that was on the floor and the girl kitten liked to sit and be admired. 'Just hard saying goodbye to Erin and starting over again, you know, school tomorrow . . .'

'Don't you like your school?'

'It's OK. It's not that,' I said as I put the laptop aside.

'And your director chappie —'

'Barry.'

'Yeah him, he likes your theme for the play, so you don't have to worry about that any more,' he said, then couldn't resist a quick burst of a Hindi song and a Bangra-type dance around the room. (Dad learned to speak Hindi when we lived in Rajasthan.) 'I will take you back to India one day. To Udaipur, where you were born. It is one of the most beautiful places on earth: mountains around a lake and the City Palace along its shores is one of the most glorious settings . . . oh but, don't look so sad.'

'I can't *help* it. I wish I was going back into school tomorrow with Erin and didn't have to go through the whole odd-girl-out thing again.'

Dad came to sit beside me and put an arm round me. With his other hand, he picked up Posh from my knee and plonked her on his. 'It's my fault, isn't it? Hauling you off around the world.'

I shrugged. 'Broadened my mind,' I said, quoting what he always used to tell us when we set off from one place to another. 'It's just . . . it's been hard to make *good* friends and having Erin here only served to remind me how much I miss her.' She'd already texted twice: once just before she got on the plane and once when she landed on the other side, and then she'd got straight on the computer as soon as she got home.

'You should have said earlier. We'd have kidnapped her. Not let her go back to Ireland.'

'Her parents might have had something to say about that!'

Dad's expression looked concerned. 'I am sorry, India. I know sometimes I've been selfish and not thought about you and how friends are *so* important, especially at your age. They can last a lifetime, and I am sure you and Erin will, but in the meantime, I'll be your friend.'

I laughed. 'Dad, are you going to come down the mall, trying on lip-gloss? Squirting on perfume samples? Come with me pulling boys? Stay up all night eating Liquorice All Sorts and talking about boys?'

'If necessary. I love Liquorice All Sorts. What colour lip-gloss do you think is me?'

Just at that moment, the doorbell rang and Dad pushed Posh aside and went to answer. A few minutes later, he came back in and announced, 'Someone to see the Cinnamon Girl.'

I turned around to see that it was Leela. She came right over and sat next to me and, like Dad had done moments ago, she plonked Posh on her knee. Posh looked at me as if to say, 'For heaven's sake, will *someone* keep still around here.'

'Hey,' said Leela.

'Hey,' I said.

'I just brought some more of the kittens' things and . . .' – she produced a little carrier bag with a ribbon on it – 'and this to say thanks for rescuing them.'

I took the present and opened the ribbon. Inside was a gorgeous pink velvet make-up bag and some rust-coloured lip-gloss. She'd got the colour I like just right. 'Wow. You didn't have to do this. I was glad to take the kittens. I love them. I've called them Posh and Becks.'

Leela laughed. 'Perfect,' she said. 'So, back to the nuthouse tomorrow, yeah?'

I nodded. 'You ready?'

'Not really. You?'

'Not really.'

'And . . . I wanted to say, I . . . I know it was private but . . . I saw the message you left in church.'

I felt my stomach tighten and I could feel myself blushing.

'Oh God, nooooo. How embarrassing.'

'No it's not. Don't be embarrassed. I thought it was sweet.'

'*Nooooo*, you must think I'm totally desperate or something.'

'Why? That's what church is for, isn't it? Saying what you need.'

'What religion is your family? I thought after seeing some of the statues around your house that you were Hindu or something.'

Leela shook her head. 'We're all something different. Gran's Hindu. So's Mum. Anisha is Buddhist. Rajiv is agnostic. Dad's Christian. The cats can't make up their minds. One is an atheist, the other is a devil-worshipper.'

I laughed. 'What are you?'

'Nudist . . . No, joking. Universal. Like, sometimes I like to go to the temple with Mum and Gran. Sometimes I like to go and sit in the church with Dad. I went with him this morning and that's when I saw your prayer.'

'How did you know the message was from me?'

'You mentioned Erin and how you'd like a friend like her, and I put two and two together. I don't know anyone else called Erin, not at our school anyhow.'

'Right. Course. I still feel embarrassed though.'

'God, don't be. I'll show you some of the messages I've left in there. Like, please let Mark Robinson notice me. Zahrah's fallen out with me, please make her call. Dear God, please let me have boobs. Size 34B if poss.'

'No!'

Leela laughed. 'Not the last one. That's my secret prayer just between you and me. I'm as flat-chested as an eight-year-old boy, and have you seen Brook and Zahrah? Like hubba hubba, mega bazongas. It's so not fair.'

I laughed. I liked Leela. She was so lucky that her friends were local.

'You look fab,' I said. 'Who needs boobs when you have a pretty face?'

'*Pff,*' she said. 'Boys like boobs. Like Mark Robinson only has eyes for chestie bits. He treats me like I'm a kid.' At that moment her phone bleeped that she had a text. She pulled it out of her pocket and glanced down at it. 'Mum. Got to go. But listen, tomorrow, if you want to hang out in the lunch break or whatever, you're welcome.'

'Me? What about Brook and Zahrah?'

'They're cool with it. We had a chat about you after you came round that day to see the kittens. We all liked you and all of us felt that we should have been more sensitive. It's rough being a new girl.'

'Are you sure? I mean are they sure?'

'Yeah. Deffo.'

'Really? Wow. Oh God, did they see my message in the church?'

Leela shook her head. 'No, and I won't tell them if you don't want. But you ought to see some of the messages *they* have left in the church, like total blackmail material.'

'Really?'

'Uhuh,' said Leela. 'Tell you about it tomorrow.'

'OK, cool,' I said as she put Posh aside, got up and went to the door.

'Thanks and . . . um, do you think you and Brook and Zahrah might like to go to a movie one night? There's some good ones around at the mo.'

'We like romantic comedies best.'

'Me too. I hate horror and violent films.'

'Me too. Rajiv loves them, but they do my head in.'

'Me too. Give me nightmares.'

'Me too.'

'OK. So. Laters.'

Leela smiled. 'Laters,' she said. 'Deffo.'

Sometimes in life, when you give up and stop trying so hard, things slip into place. Boys or friends. If you try too hard or are desperate, they evade you, I thought as I showed her out. *When you're cool and let go, they come and find you.*

After she'd gone, I went down to Mum's workroom and drew a new self-portrait for my project. I did it in bright sunshine colours. And this time, there wasn't only me in it. This time, there was me and Posh and Becks and Dad and Dylan and Mum and Aunt Sarah and Kate and Lewis and Ethan and Jessica and Lara and Eleanor and Leela and Zahrah and Brook. And Erin. And Joe. It was the kind of drawing a five-year-old kid would do, with matchstick people with big heads, but everyone was smiling.

And suddenly, when I thought about school in the morning, instead of it being daunting, starting over was full of possibilities, just waiting to be explored.

The complete Cathy Hopkins collection

The MATES, DATES series
1. Mates, Dates and Inflatable Bras
2. Mates, Dates and Cosmic Kisses
3. Mates, Dates and Portobello Princesses
4. Mates, Dates and Sleepover Secrets
5. Mates, Dates and Sole Survivors
6. Mates, Dates and Mad Mistakes
7. Mates, Dates and Pulling Power
8. Mates, Dates and Tempting Trouble
9. Mates, Dates and Great Escapes
10. Mates, Dates and Chocolate Cheats
11. Mates, Dates and Diamond Destiny
12. Mates, Dates and Sizzling Summers

Companion Books:
Mates, Dates Guide to Life
Mates, Dates and You
Mates, Dates Journal

The TRUTH, DARE, KISS OR PROMISE series
1. White Lies and Barefaced Truths
2. Pop Princess
3. Teen Queens and Has-Beens
4. Starstruck
5. Double Dare
6. Midsummer Meltdown
7. Love Lottery
8. All Mates Together

The CINNAMON GIRL series
1. This Way to Paradise
2. Starting Over
3. Looking for a Hero (Coming soon)

Find out more at www.piccadillypress.co.uk
Join Cathy's Club at www.cathyhopkins.com

Cathy Hopkins

Like this book?
Become a mate today!

Join **CATHY'S CLUB** and be the first to get the lowdown on the LATEST NEWS, BOOKS and FAB COMPETITIONS straight to your mobile and e-mail.

PLUS there's a FREE MOBILE WALLPAPER when you sign up! What are you waiting for?

Simply text MATE plus your date of birth (ddmmyyyy) to 60022 now! Or go to www.cathyhopkins.com and sign up online.

Once you've signed up keep your eyes peeled for exclusive chapter previews, cool downloads, freebies and heaps more fun stuff all coming your way.

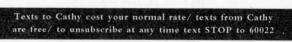

www.piccadillypress.co.uk

☆ The latest news on forthcoming books

☆ Chapter previews

☆ Author biographies

☆ Fun quizzes

☆ Reader reviews

☆ Competitions and fab prizes

☆ Book features and cool downloads

☆ And much, much more . . .

Log on and check it out!

Piccadilly Press